Abou

Sara Marchant received her MFA in Creative Writing from the University of California, Riverside/Palm Desert and teaches Critical Thinking and Writing at Mt. San Jacinto College. She lives in the high desert of Southern California with her husband, two dogs, a goat and five chickens.   @the_sara_marchant

The Driveway Has Two Sides

SARA MARCHANT

Fairlight Books

First published by Fairlight Books 2018

Fairlight Books
Summertown Pavilion,
18 - 24 Middle Way,
Oxford, OX2 7LG

A CIP catalogue record for this book is available from the British Library

1 2 3 4 5 6 7 8 9 10

ISBN 978-1-912054-42-8

www.fairlightbooks.com

Printed and bound in Great Britain by Clays Ltd, Elcograf S.p.A.

Designed by Sara Wood

Illustrated by Sam Kalda
www.folioart.co.uk

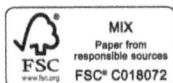

MIX
Paper from
responsible sources
FSC® C018072

For my mother.

Her name was Delilah. Or at least, that's what she told the sheriff. The village matriarchs, led by Mrs. Oakapple, said it sounded made up. It would be weeks before they learned her name, so at first, and often even afterwards, they referred to her as 'the girl'. They were taciturn by nature, and the environment on the island required tact, discretion, and independence.

An island, you see, an East Coast island. Not a West Coast or a Mediterranean island. It wasn't the tropical breeze and swaying palm tree kind. It was a tall pine moaning with the sea gusts and unexpected hurricanes hurling their way off the Atlantic kind of island. The year-round islanders were a bit sturdier than the average mainlander, tougher, but their village—there was only one on the island—they all thought was just lovely.

On this island, off Cape Cod, there was a small cottage for sale. It shared a driveway with a larger house where a man lived alone. The driveway was wide and unpaved; its gravel petered out toward the end where it segued into beach sand and sharp seagrass. The shared driveway was thought to be the reason the cottage lingered on the market; who wanted to share an inconvenient driveway?

One day in late winter, a taxi left the girl and her baggage at the cottage. She had the keys and went in. She almost immediately walked back out to prop open the door with a deckchair that had seen its best days thirty years before. The islanders were able to track the girl's movements in the house by the windows that she forced open with bangs and great exhalations of breath. The cottage had been a rental for most of its existence, and they all knew in what state renters left a place. Surreptitiously, the village housewives shook their heads in sympathy for the task the girl faced.

But if the girl *wasn't* happy, she gave no sign. She spent the first week cleaning, wearing overalls and no make-up, her black hair tied back with the type of thick white rubber band that came around the delivered newspaper. Otherwise she paced the front garden, a pen and notebook in hand. Her neighbors watched and discussed her. The man next door watched too, but he had no one with whom to discuss her. He kept himself to himself.

On the weekends, she took frequent breaks on the front porch and watched the street. It was more than a month before her waiting was rewarded. It was almost, but not quite, warm enough for her to be wearing the flouncy dress instead of her overalls on the afternoon a little sports car drove up and a city type, too old for his long hair and overly blue denim jeans, unfolded from the car to embrace her. He was tall, so tall that when he picked her up to kiss her red mouth, her dress was hitched up high on her thighs. The watching villagers disapproved. The watching neighbor did not.

The off-islanders went into the cottage, but re-appeared after a while to move the little car to the garage. The man walked the length of the shared drive, twice. He stood in the middle and surveyed both properties. Due to the placement of the buildings and the fact that it was a particularly windy day, the listeners were not able to catch what he said to the girl waiting patiently at the gate until he finished his angry inspection. They surmised he had discovered the shared driveway for the first time, but they all stopped watching when the girl distracted her man by wrapping her body around his—'In broad daylight,' Mrs. Oakapple huffed in distaste from her upstairs window—and rubbing her cheek into his neck. Well, almost everyone stopped watching. The man next door stayed at his window until the canoodling couple entered the cottage once more.

They didn't come out until the next afternoon when they took a walk on the beach. The wind threw snippets of their talk around the houses facing the water. Mostly the city man spoke phrases like '… not disclosed in the engineer's report…' and '…keep track of household budgets…' and the occasional, 'God, I've missed you.' The girl's words were lost under the waves rushing to shore and the susurration of the breeze through the seagrass that covered the dunes. The girl must have laid in a supply of food, because the couple neither shopped nor ate out. The housewives approved of this, if not the situation.

When the man left on the Monday-morning ferry, the girl returned to her activities of home repair and clearing, but now serious work began in the front garden. Dead things were ripped out, pulled back, clipped, and raked. The girl dragged the detritus to the back yard and burned it in her fire pit. She was back in overalls. Her lips were once more a pale unpainted pink, pulled into a rather fierce smile as she watched the fire burn.

She bicycled to the hardware store. Island Hardware was fairly empty, but it was early in the day. A middle-aged lady stood behind the thick wooden counter, adding up receipts. She stopped and stared at the new customer. Delilah did not approach her, merely stared back. She thought it best to let the proprietor set the tone. Thus far, the tone was awkward. Delilah didn't know how to break the silence. The lady's stare was startled, accusatory, and rather embarrassed. Delilah didn't like it at all.

'Thompson!' The lady didn't break eye contact as she called out.

From the stacks of towering merchandise, a tall stooped man appeared, his eyebrows raised at his lady. The eyebrows went higher then lowered when he spied Delilah standing, the letter of introduction from Alan's bank in her hand.

'Oh,' the man said. 'Yup. Can I help you?'

'Is there such a thing as a chainsaw that doesn't run on gasoline?' Delilah gestured delicately with the letter as she spoke.

This was inherently not the question the man, Thompson, was expecting, for his eyebrows shot up again. Simultaneously, Delilah and the man realized they both wore overalls and black rubber boots. They matched. This relaxed them. Thompson's eyebrows attained normal altitude.

'I can order you a chainsaw that uses electricity,' Thompson said. 'But I think what you need is a circular saw, and I have one in stock you can take with you.'

'Do you deliver?' Delilah asked. 'Because I need to make a big order.'

The woman, Mrs. Thompson, seemed rather more approving after hearing Delilah's news. Her arms dropped from her cross-clench and her stance relaxed.

'Yup,' Thompson said. 'We deliver.'

He beckoned her to follow him into the stacks, but Mrs. Thompson waved Delilah over to the counter. Delilah, understanding which side her bread was buttered on in the hierarchy of women, walked to her. She held out her hand for Delilah's letter and Delilah set it on the woman's open palm.

'When you're done,' Mrs. Thompson said, 'you can use the telephone to call and have your own service started. Well, gracious,' she said after she read the letter, 'I'll do it for you while you shop. Then, in the future, you can just call in an order and we'll deliver it. Save you the need to come in.'

Thompson cleared his throat as he beckoned once more for Delilah to follow him. She thought about thanking Mrs. Thompson, but decided against it. Alan's money would be thanks enough.

The order was indeed so large that Mr. Thompson called in a younger man, Thompson Junior, Delilah christened this one, to help load and deliver it. Delilah declined Junior's offer of a lift home in the cab, she needed to visit the greengrocer. She gave the proprietor there another bank letter in exchange for a wheeled wicker basket of staples and a few fresh vegetables. Delilah could see she would need to grow her own produce. Plans for this distracted her until she reached her driveway and discovered the Island Hardware truck was already unloaded. They'd put it all on the porch, but at her request, they carried some of it into the living room. She hadn't locked any doors, but apparently island men didn't try doorknobs. Being inside made them visibly nervous and they departed before Delilah could say anything other than, 'Thanks.'

Later, Delilah picked up the now in-service telephone. The rotary dial made a satisfying burr as it clicked through the numbers. She held the receiver to her ear to better hear the lines connecting.

'Island Hardware.'

'I forgot to ask you about paint,' Delilah said. 'I need gold paint.'

'Gold?' Mrs. Thompson asked. 'Did you say gold?'

'Yup.' Delilah borrowed island vocabulary. 'Like the metal.'

'Um,' Mrs. Thompson thought out loud. 'I

think we have the little tubes for craft projects.'

'No,' Delilah said. 'I need about a gallon. Paint for metalwork. Is that enamel? Maybe I should come in and talk to Mr. Thompson.'

'That's not necessary,' Mrs. Thompson snapped. Delilah wondered if the woman's professional pride was pricked or if this was some kind of wifely jealousy. 'I handle the paint inventory.'

Ah, professional pride. Delilah could understand that.

Over the next few weeks the Island Hardware truck delivered a wheelbarrow, a crowbar, and a shiny new shovel, spade, and hoe. Also, a large pile of beautifully composted garden soil. The girl danced with the shovel as she moved the soil where she needed it. From his upstairs window, the man who shared a driveway could be seen smiling.

But this was just the surface. If you looked underneath you noticed certain signs that all was not as it should be. The man next door hardly ever went out and no visitors ever went in. When he did go, it was in his own car that he kept in the garage at the front of the shared drive, and he left the island on the ferry. He made no overtures of neighborliness to the girl, and to the villagers' eyes she seemed either uninterested, or maybe not even aware of his existence. This was odd because they shared a driveway.

Also odd was the unusually frequent visits of the sheriff's cruisers to the neighborhood. They didn't stop, unless it was to tell the sparse tourists to stop parking illegally and blocking people's driveways. Sheriff Ted, when questioned, side-stepped, but the islanders pardoned any lapses by the good sheriff due to his recent bereavement.

And what about that girl? How could she afford a beachfront cottage on an island where real estate was exclusive and pricey for potting sheds? After two months she showed no sign of employment—or any sign of being independently wealthy. There were a few of those on the island, the independently wealthy; they weren't much liked. Everyone assumed the man in the house sharing a driveway with the girl was one of them.

The girl rode an old no-color bicycle she'd found in her garage. The bike had a decrepit basket wired to the front that she used for carrying groceries or small plants she bought at the nursery. She was polite to the shopkeepers, she smiled at babies and the aged, but she never engaged in conversation. 'At least she doesn't keep a cat,' said Mrs. Oakapple to Mrs. Bradshaw as they stood outside the pharmacy watching the girl pedal away. 'I can't abide a cat.'

Delilah smiled a lot while riding the bike, but not actually *at* anyone; the islanders appreciated the difference. She started a tab at the grocery and the hardware like almost every other islander, and this might have endeared her to them, but unlike the islanders the girl didn't settle up weekly or monthly when her paycheck arrived. Her monthly tab was mailed to an office address on the mainland and a check was promptly returned.

Her dress was another item of status confusion. She daily wore baggy overalls and shirts, a black swimsuit for beach swimming so old that white elastic threads waved from it, and cut-offs with a tank top for her daily morning run. Except when the boyfriend was in town, that is. Then the flouncy dresses reappeared, or the skirts, lace camisoles, and revealing two-piece swimsuits.

What was obvious was that she was happiest during the week. She smiled for the boyfriend— who drove the expensive car and showed up for the occasional weekend—and dressed in the sexy clothes and hardly ever left the cottage when he was in residence. Her lips were redder on Saturday and Sunday. But she smiled to herself on weekdays, and this smile scrunched up her eyes, and sometimes there was a smudge on her cheek all day with no one to tell her. Her hair would be in a messy ponytail, garden soil under her nails. Her attitude suggested she hummed as she worked. No islander came close enough to find out, of course. At least, not for a while.

It did not take much imagination for the watching villagers to mark the situation as sordid. A beautiful young woman—Has it been mentioned that the girl was beautiful? Or maybe that was a given—and a rich older man who provided a secluded house and a comfortable living in exchange for... what, exactly? No one *knew*, but everyone knew.

No one ever spoke to the neighbor so no one knew what his thoughts might be. There was never an opportunity to speak with the man in the yellow house. He avoided society so assiduously that eventually island society avoided him. When he drove off in his old car, heads turned in order not to see him.

Spring weather concentrated the girl's attention on the front garden. Surprising the villagers, it was planted as a kitchen garden. The cottage garden around the periphery remained, however, showing she'd some common sense. Sighs were heaved that she hadn't ripped out the mature plantings and thrown those away as well. 'She may be no better than she should be,' Mrs. Oakapple told Mrs. Thompson at the clinic's annual charitable drive, 'but at least she isn't wasteful.'

'She put a kitchen garden in her front yard,' one of the younger, less stoic housewives said to her mother. Someone capable of such heresy outside was capable of practically anything in private. 'What do you suppose the inside looks like when she's given away all the furniture?' Her mother shushed her. Admitting to curiosity was blasphemous as well.

The women of the island relaxed in silent relief when the girl in the cottage dragged the bicycle from her garage, packed a picnic in the basket, and hopped on. Clean was clean, but obsessively clean made the rest of them look bad. It was harder to keep track of her, but her sudden appearance riding through one's neighborhood kept life interesting. It was almost an honor if she paused to study your garden. Her exploration of the island led to other, unsavory situations, but the islanders weren't to know that at first.

At the other end of the girl and her neighbor's driveway, at the entrance to Mulberry Street, two sturdy yet elegantly slim posts stood embedded on either side of the gravel. Iron rings jutted out at the top of each. Delilah never saw the posts until spring began to segue into early, hopeful summer, and a few more tourists trickled onto the island, exiting the ferry.

On that afternoon she wheeled her bike from the garage, a new nursery catalogue in the basket next to her packed lunch, walked to the end of the driveway, and stopped. A length of chain was clipped to each post in order to hang down and bar entrance to the driveway. A small metal sign hung from the middle. The side facing Delilah was blank. She carefully unclipped the chain from the post on her side of the driveway, pushed the bike though, clipped the chain closed again, and then turned to read the sign. PRIVATE PROPERTY. She rode away frowning.

Blue Hydrangea

There was one garden in particular on the island that Delilah admired. It was inland, away from the sometimes-rough wind of the coast, just distant enough from the village proper that it took her a while to discover it on her swooping, unplanned, self-guided garden tour. This garden she found so lushly perfect that she did a double take riding by, and made a U-turn before stopping her bicycle and dismounting: a high compliment. She was studying the plantings and the layout from the polite distance of the front gate, when a man wearing mud boots came around the side of the house and spoke to her.

'Hello,' he said.

Delilah took a step back and stopped clutching the willow-weave garden gate. She hadn't expected him to speak to her. Those hydrangeas, though! Anyone who grew those was someone she could learn from.

'Hello,' she said, but it came out too softly. 'Hello. I was just admiring your hydrangeas.'

He smiled warmly and proudly. This gave her the courage to go on.

'Might I ask,' she said, but then started over. 'Mine are sad specimens compared to these monsters; I'd be embarrassed for you to see them.'

'It's the soil,' he said. 'Your soil is too sandy over there and I expect a little salty. Plus, the wind...'

Delilah stiffened. He knew where she lived? Who she was? Small town, small island, she reminded herself, and relaxed. Perhaps all hydrangeas on the island were buffeted by salt-breeze and malnourished by sandy soil. Maybe he alone held the cure.

'Could I amend it?' she asked. 'The soil? Any advice?'

His eyes widened, but not in a surprised way. Delilah knew that look. She'd asked an older man to explain something to her, give his wise counsel. Inwardly, she sighed in resignation and relief. They were so easy, she thought.

He invited her through the gate into his garden. Up close he was old enough to be her father. His hair was not blond, as she'd judged from a distance, but gray. Although most of the islanders passed the age of twenty possessed crow's feet from squinting in the glare, he had more. The lines around his mouth looked like the residue of laughter, but laughter that ended a while ago. He looked tired. He looked sad. Delilah sighed again. This resignation contained no relief.

The man led the girl through his garden. They lingered by the hydrangeas massed against the front of his saltbox home, but she was entranced by a wisp of an odor—spicy, exotic—and he showed her around back to his Cedar of Lebanon.

'So beautiful,' Delilah said, inhaling. She gazed up at the lacy branches and then back down to earth. She studied the multi-hued green lawn dappled by the branches' dancing shade. 'And so peaceful.'

Nothing was in flower yet, spring was so new, but Delilah knew her leaves and her greens, her trees and her shrubs. Her eye saw what *was* and her mind filled in what *would* be.

There were silvery-blue hosta, the black foliage of crape myrtle and specialized mallow, the fiery orange-red of the native *Carpinus caroliniana*, but the variety of green was equally spectacular. Here was the glossy deep magnolia, the dusty gray of a weeping blue atlas cedar—not as scented as the nearby Cedar of Lebanon, but fascinating with its contorted shape draped over a rotting split-rail fence slowly bowing to time and the growing cedar's weight. The shades and variations of green, high-lighted by the specimen plants that were not green, looked more than natural. They looked supernatural. It was an Impressionist painting come to life. It was a masterpiece. Ted was an artist. Delilah wanted to take his hand, acolyte-like, and kiss it. She stepped further away from him in consequence.

'I've been spending most of my time here,' he said at that moment. 'Since my wife died I don't seem to want to do much else.'

Delilah looked at him, quickly, up from her fingering of an artemisia bush. Her eyes read his face, but she didn't speak. She didn't offer condolences. The bitter scent of the crushed white leaves swirled on the slight breeze that reached this far inland.

'This place gets all my attention,' he said when he realized she wasn't going to ask questions or offer any words of polite sympathy. 'That is, when I'm not working for the town.'

Delilah looked the question at him, rubbing the sprig of artemisia she'd broken off the shrub over her closed lips.

'I'm the sheriff,' Ted told her. He said it shyly, not used to announcing his profession. Usually, it was known.

He saw her recoil and he wondered at it. Her shock held a subtle scent of fear. But why should she fear him? Her living situation was perhaps immoral if you asked some of the island's old biddies, but it wasn't illegal. Her shock, and the flash of fear, was almost immediately suppressed. He could have told himself he'd imagined it, but he hadn't. He was old enough to be tired of those games, and sheriff long enough to trust his hair-on-the-back-of-the-neck instincts. Human beings would always go further than one could previously have believed them capable of going.

That's it, Ted thought. *She'll flee this interview and never return.* He'd only see her during the routine drive-by he and his lone deputy made. He would never host her in his garden again, although maybe for his shrubs' sake that was a good thing. She'd roughed up his artemisia. Ted realized the thought of never seeing her again among his garden's beauty made him sad. He was being ridiculous. She was a visitor here, there was no expectation of friendship, and she was young enough that authority made her nervous.

Then he saw a strange thing. Delilah's posture changed. She took a deep breath, held it, and then released it. She put the crushed sprig in her pocket and smiled up at Ted wryly. He was confused, but relieved. She was prettier than all his plants put together—more beautiful even than his prize *Rosa rugosa* that covered the trellis next to the screened porch. Then the girl said something that went straight to Ted's heart.

'What color are the hydrangea's flowers?'

'Blue,' he said. She smiled, and he smiled back at her pleasure.

They discussed pH balancing of the soil that turned the multi-flowered globes the deep cyanotic blue as they strolled across the plush lawn behind his house to the kitchen garden.

Later, during his trips by her house, Ted watched as she developed her kitchen garden in the front. He understood her reasoning; there was more room, more sun, a fence to use as garden bones. He still found it scandalous, yet also intriguing, he had to admit.

There was a proper method of hanging laundry on a line, here on the island—taught by mothers to daughters. Private items of clothing went on the innermost lines, sheets and towels on the outside; even clean laundry wasn't for public view. This girl had taken a circular saw to her laundry line out back and then burned the wood. But she planted the garden that supplied her food in full view of anyone passing.

What more was she capable of? Ted had to wonder as he showed her his kitchen garden hidden from all eyes but his own, at the back of his property, screened from the road. This was the proper placement of a vegetable bed to Ted's way of thinking, but he was careful not to share this thought with her.

By the end of the tour, near the rows of baby cabbages and the silver-green leathery leaves of not-yet-flowering eggplants, he liked the girl. He would be sorry if she didn't come back. Again, he was old enough not to kid himself that her loveliness and her scent of honey mixed with freshly turned loam didn't add to her attraction. But mostly it was just nice to talk to someone as obsessed with gardening as he was.

She did come back. It took a week, but she did. He'd loaned her a book about composting and some old issues of *Horticulture* magazine, and she was returning them. Ted was touched when he saw slips of paper between the pages. She'd taken notes and wanted to discuss questions specific to the island's climate, soil, and seasonal changes.

The sheriff was surprised and pleased. He invited her into the kitchen. He'd only imagined the flash of fear during her first visit, he told himself. Her slight hesitation before she entered his house he put down to a thorough wiping of her sneakered feet on his hedgehog shoe brush.

He made tea and served scones given to him by his deputy's mother. Since his wife's death, the sheriff had taken for granted such gifts from the island's womenfolk, especially the single ladies of a certain age, and he barely noticed when the gifts of baked goods slacked off shortly after the girl's third visit.

The third time she arrived unannounced *(Had she never had a telephone installed? Ted should look into that.)* she brought thick drawing paper and colored pencils. She was teaching herself to make garden plans. Would he mind if she practiced on his? Ted blushed, then laughed at his blush. A tea party was held on the white wrought-iron table and chairs Ted's wife had bought and he'd always considered froufrou. They sat near the arborvitae, shaded by the delicious-smelling Cedar of Lebanon, but it was a beautiful day without wind, and many people out walking and biking witnessed their sheriff and the girl engaged in... whatever it was that they were engaged in. Their heads were bowed over the paper-covered table as they passed the colored pencils back and forth. Whatever it was, it looked intimate.

Normally, the sheriff was attuned to the general

mood of the citizenry; a man in his position had to be. When the food baskets stopped, however, he barely questioned it. The women no longer feeding him, well, maybe there was an etiquette-sanctioned cut-off date for the feeding of widowers. The attitude of the men he really should have seen, he thought later. There was no excuse, he mused. Men of his generation became almost respectful in an odd, envious manner. Men of a younger generation, the girl's generation, were one step away from hostile. These men took their speeding or parking tickets, their warnings about loud music at the beach, the confiscation of their open bottles of alcohol, with resentment muffled by years of ingrained respect for his station.

The sheriff should have noticed all this and drawn conclusions, and perhaps addressed the issue, but he didn't. By the time the women stopped feeding him completely—the baked goods ended first, the casseroles trickled gradually to a stop because the island's thrifty housewives found it a convenient way to dispose of leftovers—he was sleeping with the girl when she came to talk gardens. When men his age paid him the dubious compliment of envy, he was already in love with her. Even if he had realized the young men took the tickets from his hand with contemptuous resentment because he'd dared to do what none of them had—and succeeded—it wouldn't have mattered. It was too late.

After a while, the sheriff's garden was no longer picture-perfect. In fact, the edges were distinctly raggedy. Sometimes plants were actually wilting before he watered them. He didn't notice that, either, so busy was he, so obsessed, with tending to the girl, and by extension, her garden. He'd have been amazed by any accusations of seduction. He'd no intention of such.

It was a very wet spring, the roads were muddy, and Delilah had no car. She wore her overalls and mud boots to his house. Another thing he should have noticed from the beginning, she discouraged him from visiting her cottage. He'd never been inside. He'd cruise by on patrol and eyeball her garden, he felt he knew each plant as a friend, but only because of her detailed garden plan. He'd never walked her garden. It wasn't until called upon to settle Delilah's driveway injuries that he even set boots on her property.

It was softly raining again that day, the first day they were truly together. She arrived on her bicycle. Her floppy rain hat and yellow slicker kept her from being sopping, but her boots were muddy and the legs of her overalls were dark with moisture. She looked more than uncomfortable. She reminded

Ted of a cat he'd fished from the lagoon once: too miserable to bare its claws. Ted waved Delilah into the mudroom before he took her hat and coat.

When he turned away for the towel he kept warming over the radiator for just such a purpose, he heard the clasps on her overalls click open. He turned just as she stepped from her clothing, easy as breathing. She placed the wet denim on the radiator and gave Ted a moment to collect himself.

She still wore her long-sleeved cotton shirt; this one was pink faded by the sun and came to mid-thigh. Her thick socks were the color of brown sugared oatmeal. One foot rested upon the other as she waited for Ted to invite her into the kitchen. Ted was pretty sure that everything he could see was all that she wore. He cleared his throat and invited her through the door.

'You're probably cold,' he said. 'I'll make tea.'

She sat at the table, still toweling her hair. She'd undone her braid and the damp length of it curled as it dried. They drank the tea while looking over her newest garden plan. The back garden's emptiness was exciting her. This plan, her latest, was still in its infancy, but there was so much nothing to work with. The front garden had been so full of someone else's dream that she'd been forced to improvise around. That had its interesting aspects and challenges too, of course. 'Using another's vision to craft your own? I've done that,' Delilah said. 'But the back? Hidden almost? That's all mine.'

Ted only nodded. He understood the joy of growing new life, creating beauty where none existed before, but he didn't follow what he saw as her... territoriality? But then he was awfully distracted by the way she was sitting with her knees folded under her on the chair, leaning on her elbows on the table to run a long finger down the line on the plan representing the shared driveway.

Her shirt rode up her thighs and she shivered. She wasn't the only one. It only seemed natural to offer her his warm bathrobe. Or maybe a blanket. His pajamas?

'You're cold,' Ted said. He stood up. 'Come on.'

She followed him to the bedroom where his dead wife's clothes hung in the closet, but somehow, instead of Delilah putting on more clothing, she ended up with less. She did have underpants on under the pink shirt, after all. They were pink, too. Pink lace panties that matched her pink lace bra, and she dropped both items to make a crumpled pile on the floor with her socks. It was the last time he ever saw them, or anything of their ilk. After that first time, she always had on sensible white cotton underwear. But he didn't notice that, either.

The Herb Garden

The day Delilah found her driveway chained and marked with that disturbing **PRIVATE PROPERTY** sign, she was thankful she'd laid claim to Ted. The chain, the sign, and its message flabbergasted her. Did the sign include her? Did the chain? But it was her property, too. She possessed a deed entitled so. She looked forward to discussing this new development with Ted; it fell squarely in his wheelhouse, so to speak.

One of the reasons she preferred older men was that she felt they understood that when she asked for advice or opinion, it was because they were mature. They'd lived longer so they knew more. Men her own generation assumed they could give advice just because they were men. This was the sort of stupidity that drove Delilah nuts. As her grandmother used to say: the devil isn't wise because he's the devil; he's wise because he is so old. Delilah never shared this with Ted nor Alan. She doubted

Ted would appreciate being compared to the devil and Alan would openly sulk at being called old.

Delilah made the long bicycle ride to Ted's side of the island.

Ted wasn't home, but there was a note on the kitchen table. He didn't lock his door. No one on the island locked their doors except during mid-summer when all the tourists ran amok, but Delilah didn't know this yet and thought Ted left his door unlocked for her, which caused her heart to swell with something like gratitude, love, and pretty-girl complacency all rolled into one.

Ted was called into an emergency budget meeting, the note read, but would call her later if she couldn't stay and wait. Delilah chuckled over the island having budget problems—the property taxes Alan paid on her behalf were extraordinary—and then started the ride home. She'd been postponing the back garden revitalization, but tonight she'd postpone no longer. She felt the need for some bracing manual labor. That chain and its sign unsettled her.

It was still there, and she entered with the same deliberation that she'd used when she'd exited. She glanced irritably up at the neighboring yellow house, instigator of the sign. As per usual it looked empty. She put the bike in her garage and brought out the shovel, a crowbar, and her wheelbarrow. She dressed for gardening every day because she never knew when she might have to drop to her knees and pull a weed, or grab the clippers and trim back a rampaging shrub.

The back garden area was paved, sort of, with large, irregularly shaped sandstone slabs. This was a travesty to Delilah. She'd removed the broken barbeque equipment in the dark of winter, and only a few sad willows grew at the edges of the fence line, no doubt blown in by the wind and self-seeded. Delilah intended to remove the flagstones to the front where she wanted a path amongst the planted beds, and have the space, here, to turn the neglected patch into an herb garden with perhaps a small table and chairs for a private breakfast area. But the paving had to go.

She used the shovel to loosen the soil around the closest stone before shoving the crowbar under the edge and jumping on the other end with her entire body weight. After, she was never exactly sure what happened, but there was noise and pain. When her ears stopped ringing and her vision adjusted, she found herself on the ground, in the graveled drive. Her hand was bleeding from a gash by the thumb. Her right pants leg was ripped open and her exposed shin oozed blood from shredded skin. Her tail bone blazed hellfire pain. She tried to pick gravel from the palm not bleeding, but her hand was shaking too badly, and it was only then that she realized the voice yelling, 'Are you crazy?' was not inside her head, but coming from above it.

Delilah tried to turn at the waist to face the yellow house, lost her balance from the shooting pain in her coccyx, and fell upon her back in the gravel. From this position she saw the window was open in the wall of the yellow house, the screen was dangling free from three corners, and her neighbor's head protruded. He was yelling.

'Are you crazy?' he yelled again, perhaps seeing the glazed look on her face. 'Are you trying to kill yourself? Those stones are too heavy for you! What are you thinking? Or are you thinking at all, idiot?'

His head disappeared into the house, and Delilah closed her eyes in relief. He seemed maybe ten years her senior. Not enough. Not nearly enough.

'Here!' He was back, yelling. Delilah's eyes opened in time to see something white flutter from his hand. 'Normal people call a handyman for help. This is the guy who put up the chain. Call him!'

He pulled his head back in, and she was pretty sure he called her an idiot again as he did so. He fixed the screen in place, but didn't shut the window. Delilah closed her eyes.

'Hey,' he called again. 'Hey!'

'What!' she said, eyes still closed.

'Are you okay? Did you hit your head?'

She opened her eyes and slowly got to her feet. Limping to where the white business card lay in the gravel, she picked it up and limped back toward her side of the driveway.

'Hey,' he called again.

'I'm fine,' she yelled up to him. 'Thanks for your concern. Thanks for the card. Now piss off.'

The neighbor laughed. Or maybe it was more of a snicker. It was immediately silenced by the slamming of the window, but she heard it. She told Ted about this interaction when he called. He seconded the neighbor's recommendation of the handyman. Delilah would call the number after the bruises faded and the gash under her thumb was sufficiently healed. It was all too embarrassing.

It was bad enough telling Alan when he visited that weekend. Delilah was in the bathtub when he arrived and searched the house for her. By the time he entered the bathroom he was annoyed; he was accustomed to being greeted at the front gate by a sweet-scented, cosmetically enhanced girlfriend holding a gin and tonic.

'Oh, hi,' Delilah said from her slouched position in the hot water, and she waved with the hand not in the tub. It was clumsily bandaged.

'What happened to you?' Alan walked in and looked for a place to sit. Too large for the rattan hamper and too fastidious to use the closed toilet lid, he settled for clasping his hands as he waited.

'Help me up?' Delilah shifted to stand.

Alan did. He took her uninjured hand as she stepped carefully over the high enamel edge onto the powder-blue bathmat. She reached for the towel over the radiator, but gasped in pain. Alan didn't cover her or help her with the towel he was so enthralled with examining the bruises, scrapes, and cuts on her body. She stood still and allowed it.

'What happened to you?' There was no annoyance in his voice, only simple horror, and for the first time Delilah allowed herself to wonder if maybe he loved her a little.

'It was a gardening mishap,' Delilah said. 'I'm worried something is broken here, though.' She put a hand to the end of her spine and turned around to show him.

She then had to stand panting for a moment until the sharp stab in her coccyx dulled to a sickening throb.

'Yes,' she said. 'Broken.'

Alan wrapped a towel around her, finally. 'Let's get you dressed,' he said. 'You're cold.'

'My nightgown.' Delilah pointed to the gown on its hook behind the door.

'Bed?' Alan asked when she was dressed in flannel and he'd put her slippers on her feet.

'I'm hungry,' she said. 'Help me downstairs?'

They discovered she could only walk slowly or stand. Otherwise she was in pain enough for tears. Cooking was beyond her, sitting impossible. She stretched out on the divan in the front room while Alan rummaged for a snack. He returned to sit on the rug next to her, helping her to sip tea and eat burned toast. He did this awkwardly and seemed nervous. Delilah put her head down on a hard sofa pillow and shut her eyes.

'You can tell me about your week,' she said. 'I'm listening.'

Alan finished his tea before clearing his throat. Delilah opened her eyes to find him studying her face. He traced a path from eyes to chin and up again; like searching for clues. When she tried to smile reassuringly—*Yes, it's me*—she failed, tears leaked and ran across her lips instead. Alan looked out through the open door where the rosemary bushes were beating against the white porch railings from the force of the wind.

'I was having lunch on Friday, in the neighborhood of our old apartment,' he said. 'Just a quick bite after a meeting and I bumped into Teresa's brother on the street. Literally bumped shoulders with Louis right on the doorstep of the old apartment.'

He paused to check her reaction. She didn't have one. He went back to watching the wind throw rosemary branches around outside.

'All I could think was, what if we hadn't moved? What if we hadn't decided we needed the privacy here and you wanted more land?' Alan coughed. 'It was an odd moment, seeing Louis there.'

Delilah shut her eyes once more, listening to the wind. If she concentrated, she could hear the pounding of the waves beyond the dunes, behind the wind. She didn't respond to Alan's odd moment. She had nothing to offer.

Delilah stayed on the divan that night while Alan slept in the golden bed upstairs. In the morning, Sunday, he told her he was unsettled due to the interaction with his brother-in-law on the street in front of Delilah's old apartment. She found it telling that it was no longer 'their' apartment, but only 'her' apartment. Alan felt he should return early, make sure Teresa was not suspicious. After all, Delilah was not really up for company. She asked him nicely to bring her a loose dress before he left. She couldn't face the stairs.

She was dialing Ted's number before the roar of Alan's Porsche faded down the road. Ted arrived at the cottage as Alan was driving onto the ferry. Both of Delilah's neighbors watched from their respective upstairs windows as the sheriff helped a limping Delilah into his vehicle. It was a quiet day after that, filled with luminous sunlight behind cloudy skies and the gently wafting scent of bruised rosemary drifting up to lonely watchers.

Ted gave Delilah a lift to the island's clinic. He ignored the faces of the other patrons in the waiting room as, due to his position, he and Delilah were escorted directly to the doctor. When he would have stepped out of the room, she clutched his hand. After, he took Delilah to his house and let her cry a little, and didn't laugh at her indignant re-telling of her conversation with the neighbor. Of her visit with Alan, she offered no details.

Ted sat on the edge of the bed, holding a glass of water and one of the muscle relaxants Dr. Papadopoulos prescribed for Delilah. Ted had called on his deputy to pick it up because he wanted to get Delilah settled at home. At the back of his mind Ted realized this was as inappropriate as cutting in line at the clinic; both acts were an abuse of his station, and his home wasn't Delilah's. He pushed the thought away. Delilah's home was paid for by another man who Ted ruthlessly refused to think of for fear it would lead to other, possibly illegal, definitely abuse-of-power type thoughts.

He brushed the silky hair out of Delilah's tear-damp eyes and set the glass of water down. He'd deal with any consequences of having Deputy Hayes doing his personal errands. Ted was the sheriff; sometimes sheriffs needed help. 'Needs must when the devil drives,' Ted said.

'Where to?' Delilah's pill was kicking in.

'Never mind,' he said.

'Who is he?' Delilah said.

'The devil?' Ted smiled. She was awfully cute when she was dopey.

'No,' she said, her teeth gritted. She curled into a pained ball on her side, pulled the covers up to her chin. 'My neighbor.'

'They say he's some kind of criminal,' Ted said softly, as if he might be overheard by the man in question. 'Mrs. Oakapple and her ladies say, I mean. "Either the drugs or the guns or the Mafia with that one, Sheriff, mark my words." But no one knows, it's all just gossip.'

'What about me?' Delilah asked. Her eyes, lids swollen from her tears, were closed. Her eyelashes rested on her cheeks they were so long.

Ted stroked her arm the way his mother had stroked his when soothing him as a small, sick boy; the way Ted had stroked his dying wife's arm until she'd been in so much pain from the cancer eating her insides that she couldn't stand to be touched. He didn't want to tell Delilah what the town's matriarchs and the town's gossips—there was overlap between the groups but they were not the same—said of Delilah.

He wouldn't speak of it and that told her all she needed to know. She blinked slowly and carefully as he met her gaze; they each concealed thoughts that they would never willingly share. Ted would never hurt her, never, he told himself. It was more like a prayer.

Of Delilah's 'profession' the islanders may not approve, but at least they understood it. Her neighbor? No one even knew his name, and his lack of occupation was downright sinister. What did he do all day, and all night, in that yellow house? Ted found his existence interesting, but aside from the neighborhood drive-bys in the cruiser, left him alone.

The islanders' tendency was toward speculation, suspicion, and gossip. Actual interference was frowned upon. Delilah, her bruised ego as painful as her broken tailbone and cut thumb, appreciated the distinction. She turned over in Ted's bed, closed her eyes, and sought rest.

It was Ted who solved the backyard paving predicament. They were lying in bed that evening, listening to the early summer rain falling on the elephant ears, alliums, and camellia outside his bedroom window, when the idea hit him.

'Not all the flagstones,' he said, arms behind his head. 'Remove every other stone and plant the herbs in the empty spaces.'

Delilah, who had been idly finger-combing her overgrown black bangs, was not even momentarily confused. She carefully rearranged her legs and sat up; this was painful, but not tear-inducing. Those muscle relaxants really worked. The sheets were on the floor so she didn't bother trying to cover up.

'Eventually the herbs will grow over the edges of the stones, too. And in the meantime, a little natural mulch will help amend the soil!' In her excitement, she grabbed one of his biceps with both hands and shook it in gratitude.

After a while they got up to consult the garden books about herbs hardy enough to withstand foot traffic and garden furniture. They drank mint tea on the screened-in porch. Delilah wore Ted's bathrobe although the porch faced the backyard with its concealing veil of old, dark pines that protected them from the collective gaze of the villagers.

Delilah didn't invite Ted into her cottage. The day he'd picked her up and driven her to the clinic there were special circumstances. It was an emergency that fell under his official purview as sheriff. It wasn't like the island had an ambulance. But inviting him into the house that Alan provided for her? That she could not do. It wouldn't be right.

She was dying to show the cottage off, really she was. She'd done so much work and had no one to appreciate her efforts. Alan didn't count. He politely listened and pretended to take an interest, but she could see the boredom lurking in the corner of his eyes and she let the iteration of her weekly accomplishments trickle to a close.

Alan arrived that Friday cross and disheveled from the journey. It was a crush getting out of the city. Traffic was miserable and the Porsche was making a worrisome noise. His wife had called him that afternoon and he'd told his secretary to tell Teresa he'd already left. The look this earned him from his secretary was also worrisome.

Delilah went through the motions of soothing a fractious male. She gave him a drink—today's glass held Scotch on two cubes of ice—picked up the clothes he discarded and folded them neatly over the ladder-back chair she'd refinished for this very purpose. A salad was waiting for him and omelets would be whipped up in a jiffy. She listened to his woes with sufficient sympathy but no pity, because no man wishes to be pitied,

47

and waited until he'd completely relaxed to start telling him about her week.

But he merely seemed puzzled. He wasn't interested in her achievements: the curtains she'd sewn, the plumbing problem she'd repaired herself, the blind mole she'd accidentally caught in a gopher trap and put out of its injured misery before shoving it back into the gopher hole to show him what he'd caused. Delilah realized Alan was puzzled because she'd never before attempted to share her life without him *with* him.

Alan, always the gentleman, waited for her to stop talking so that he could start. Delilah, startled by her mistake, obliged him. For a moment she wondered if she were a real person to Alan. Did he see her as one of the porcelain dolls he bought Teresa when he traveled? When he was gone did he think Delilah stood on a shelf in the spare bedroom, collecting dust, her black hair Barbie-doll smooth, her brown eyes painted open? The anger Delilah felt at this shocked her. She stopped wondering, she stopped trying to see herself through Alan's eyes. It scared her.

To calm her mind, she began to list her changes to the cottage. She took before and after photographs in her mind, and she placed imaginary captions beneath them describing the miracles of interior decoration she'd performed. She didn't acknowledge that it wasn't Alan or even Ted to whom she addressed this internal monologue.

Alan carried on expounding and eating, then lounged on the bed and never noticed Delilah was there only physically. As she went about cleaning up Alan's mess before preparing to join him in bed, her interior conversation continued.

If only he'd seen what it looked like the day she'd moved in! (Who *he* was, she wouldn't think about. He wasn't Alan, nor was he Ted. Best not to think about it at all.) Alan bought the cottage sight unseen; of course he'd had inspection reports and realtor photographs, he was a successful businessman after all. But the mess! And the weird piles of furniture crammed in! And the sand that had been tracked in by thirty years of renter's feet and apparently never swept back out again. Really, people were awful, Delilah thought. But she thought it silently, as she joined Alan in the bed.

Alan supported her because she was nice to look at, fun to be around, had no interest in going public, and possessed a vivid sensual nature coupled with a complete lack of inhibition. Delilah had no ambition in life higher than growing a beautiful garden and maintaining a home of domestic comfort. Maybe Alan appreciated this as much as he did the other aspects of their relationship, the carnal ones. But he wasn't actually interested in learning how she obtained these domestic comforts. Delilah kept them to herself until Monday arrived, Alan left, and she was able to call Ted. He was such a good listener.

Ted couldn't help her with the labor of building the herb garden, of course. He couldn't come on the property, much less pitch in and work on Alan's territory. It wouldn't be decent. Delilah was forced to hire a handyman; the one whose card fluttered down from her rude neighbor's window. He was the only handyman on the island it seemed. But it was to Ted that Delilah gave a day-by-day progress report, and it was with Ted she celebrated the herb garden's completion, drinking lemon balm tea and eating cookies in bed. His bed.

Perhaps Delilah noticed that the progression of the herb garden's creation was watched over by the neighbor in the yellow house. Maybe she saw the handyman raise a hand in acknowledgment of a former employer once or twice as he worked. If she did see the man with whom she shared a driveway when he glanced her way out through his window, she never mentioned it to Ted. And she was very careful to never raise her black-haired head from her tasks. She wanted no accidental meeting of glances. She talked to her

neighbor only in her head. She kept herself to
herself.

The Yellow House

Anton was in exile. Anton was in exile on a small, lonely island in a large, drafty house with terrible lighting. Anton couldn't stop thinking of Napoleon lately. 'Able was I ere I saw Elba.' But this island wasn't Elba and Anton wasn't Napoleon. He had to stop thinking like that.

Anton wasn't Napoleon; he didn't want to conquer the world. Anton wasn't even John Dillinger. He hadn't killed anybody or extorted money from anybody or driven anybody around who had either murdered or extorted money. Anton had merely worked in a restaurant where people who murdered or extorted money liked to eat, and one night a few years ago Anton had witnessed something many people, including Anton, would have preferred he not witness.

One of the groups of people who didn't fall into this category, the FBI agents trying to build a RICO case against the restaurant patrons, persuaded Anton (who hadn't always been named Anton) that it was in his best interests to turn state's evidence, and then disappear. Which is why Anton was exiled to this island; a protagonist in a story no one would believe were Anton able to tell it to them. He was trying to write that story. He was writing a book.

It was pointless to write the book, Anton knew, because his keepers would never allow him to publish it. It was pointless to write the book, but he was doing so anyway. Mostly he was writing the book because the island where Anton was exiled had nothing like a restaurant. There was a small coffee shop, an old fashioned ice cream shoppe, a candy store open only in the summer for the tourists' kids, and the drugstore counter that sold sandwiches; but there wasn't what Anton would call a restaurant. Islanders went to the mainland for any 'fancy' dining.

Anton had thought about opening a restaurant. During his first lonely days of exile, he'd dragged himself out of his damp bedroom with plans of opening a true Italian grotto of a restaurant. Anton planned the full stereotype for the islanders. Red-flocked wallpaper, black-and-white tiled floors, gold-painted chairs or black velvet-lined booths—maybe some of each. Every table would have a netted wine-bottle candleholder and the waitresses would wear loosely tied peasant blouses with full-tiered skirts. Preferably, Anton would have them all barefoot and languid to the point of rude, but he knew it didn't matter. He knew all his plans were for nothing.

The plans grew more elaborately strange and implausible as his first winter gloamed on because Anton knew these plans would never come to fruition. A restaurant would be the first place the murdering extorters would look for him. A restaurant was Anton's natural setting. Lions lived on the veldt, sharks swam in the sea, and Anton belonged in a dim, smoky restaurant. Therefore, Anton was writing a book. It had a lot of recipes, his book, but it wasn't a cookbook. He called it a memoir. A memoir that talked about food. A lot.

In the meantime, Anton ran. Sometimes he ran twice a day if the words didn't come. Sometimes there were problems with the house, the drafty, dark, ugly yellow house (Elba), and Anton would call one of the approved numbers taped next to the phone in the kitchen. Otherwise Anton only saw people, talked to people, when he drove to the mainland—the ancient Renault riding the ferry like a child's bathtub toy—to shop for groceries and check in with his assigned marshal.

Anton loved grocery shopping. He hated meeting his marshal.

Anton had been in exile for almost two years when the girl moved in next door. The cottage was on the market. The marshal seemed irritated by this fact when Anton moved in, but not worried. The cottage was a rental before Anton's time, but for sale it sat empty and forlorn. Anton had the posts and chain installed in the driveway during his first summer because the tourists parking in the driveway under his office window made him nervous, and the cars blocking access to his garage, and therefore his trip to the mainland, enraged him.

Anton called the marshal-approved handyman, had the posts and chain added, and forgot about the empty cottage. Until the day the black-haired girl moved in. Anton stopped thinking about Napoleon that day and started feeling like a character closer to Rapunzel. He liked that feeling even less.

The black-haired girl was also a runner. Anton would pass her occasionally, his eyes meeting hers much against his will. She was beautiful, sexy, a little goofy, but not remotely friendly. Anton told himself this was for the best. His next-door neighbor, this person who mysteriously appeared as if from nowhere, was not someone he should get involved with. 'Don't shit where you eat,' Anton's nonna would have advised him. So he didn't. But it was advisable to keep an eye on her. After all, what did he know about the intriguing dark beauty next door? She could be a mob assassin. It was unlikely, being as she only cleaned and gardened and rode the nasty bike she found in her garage. She didn't even know he, Anton, was alive, let alone seem interested in killing him. It was enough to hurt his feelings.

But one morning during his run she met his eyes with her big, dark own. After that there was maybe a head nod of acknowledgment. Later on, Anton glimpsed a smile on her face when he sneezed so hard he broke stride and the waves splashed his shoes. She would find that funny, he supposed. She really was quite goofy. And gorgeous, damn it. When she smiled, he missed another step.

Even sweaty, no make-up, her hair tied in a sloppy ponytail with one of those thick rubber bands that held broccoli stems together, when she smiled she was so beautiful Anton was tempted to break the rules and stop running. He wanted to speak to her. He wanted to know her name. He wanted to hear her voice again. He stopped this line of thinking and headed home.

However lonely in his exile, Anton knew better than to start something he couldn't finish. Anton made sure he never mentioned his new neighbor's existence to his marshal during his weekly visit. The marshal would have questions, and questions would lead to investigations, and possibly that could lead to Anton moving or somehow losing sight of his beautiful, black-haired neighbor. As much as Anton hated Elba, now that he'd found his Josephine he didn't want to leave.

He had no plans to speak to her, ever. He knew her voice was raspy, it was smoke-flavored whiskey and hot cocoa with a pinch of chili powder. Her voice was dangerous. It was enough just to watch her. She was so entertaining in her methodical-verging-on-obsessional way. He'd never seen anyone clean as much as the girl did. Her name was Delilah.

Anton heard the screen door slam one Saturday morning. Normally she was quiet in her movements, now that she'd finished destroying the furniture. She made no noise unless the man was around. Anton stepped to the window to look down into the back garden. Her arms were full, that's why the door slammed shut behind her. She held two brown paper bags, one spilling ears of corn, one empty, and a large saucepan.

'You overbought,' Anton muttered. No two

people could eat that much corn, and most people didn't cook it properly anyway. The girl sat on the lowest step and began shucking the corn, dropping the naked ears into the tall stock-pot.

'No, no, no,' Anton whispered. She was going to boil it. This was just bad. Anton would peel the husks down, but not off. He'd remove the silk carefully, rub the exposed kernels with butter and seasoning before rewrapping it in the husks and roasting the corn over tired coals.

The black-haired girl was placing the husks and silk in the empty paper bag. She performed this job neatly, gracefully, but with none of the joy she exhibited when gardening.

'Delilah!' a voice yelled from inside the cottage. Anton leaped away from the window only to almost immediately leap back in order not to miss any action. The girl was startled, too. She dropped the corn she was holding. It bounced down the steps to land in the patchy grass.

'Delilah, where are my shoes?'

Anton knew it was her boyfriend. He knew the man existed, was there that weekend, of course. Hence the absurd amount of corn. Delilah would never be that wasteful. Anton didn't like the boy-friend. Witness the idiot's inability to find his own shoes. Anton preferred to pretend the man didn't exist. This was difficult when he kept yelling.

'Delilah!'

'Find your own damn shoes,' Anton said.

As if she heard this, Delilah looked up at his window where he stood watching her. Shocked by the connection of their gaze, he froze. With their eyes locked, he read the thoughts written on her face. She was also thinking, *Find your own damn shoes.* Anton knew it sure as he knew his name. Well, no. The name was not his. He knew what Delilah was thinking sure as he remembered the yeasty smell of his nonna's sourdough bread. He and Delilah had been staring into each other's eyes for so long now Anton was uncomfortable. Wasn't he?

He dropped the curtain and stepped back. That was creepy. No doubt she thought so, too. Anton had moved a cot into his office. Not exactly because it overlooked the shared driveway; this side of the house was warmer, drier. His bedroom and living room were on the damp, dark side of the yellow house. The kitchen was on the warm, dry side. He practically lived in the kitchen, anyway. The kitchen led to the deck where he ate breakfast when it was sunny, drank wine when it was dusk, and sat to put on or take off his running shoes. Anton had more enthusiasm for living now that Delilah was next door. But he had no intention of talking to her.

All his best intentions flew out the window he opened in order to yell at her the day he watched Delilah almost brain herself with a crowbar. It was the same day he'd put up the driveway chain for the season. Tourists were beginning to arrive on the island by way of the ferry and Anton had that morning, before his run, clipped the chain with its sign to the concrete posts. After his run he'd taken his breakfast, blueberry muffins with flaxseed he'd baked earlier, to the office window overlooking the driveway. He kept a comfortable chair far enough from the window so as to rest his feet on the sill, be able to look out, and yet not be seen. Anton's book lay abandoned on the desk. It was dusty.

Anton watched Delilah fetch her bike, discover the chain and read the sign before riding away. Lately when she left on her rides she'd be gone for hours, so Anton went downstairs to clean the kitchen and do some laundry. When he heard the chain rattle Delilah's return, he peered out the kitchen window in time to see her disappear into the garage. She emerged with garden implements and Anton raced back upstairs to his viewing chair.

She was digging around one of the large stones

that paved the backyard. That was weird, but then she was the same girl who chopped down her laundry line poles for a bonfire. When she dropped the shovel and picked up the crowbar, jamming the flat edge under the stone, Anton found himself on his feet. His cup of coffee hit the floor. He made it to the window when, down below, Delilah threw all her weight on the crowbar. Anton didn't have time to open the window before the stone's greater weight countered Delilah's and she was flung backward. The stone scraped her leg as it landed back in its place, the crowbar jerked from Delilah's grasp. Her slight body hit the gravel butt first, and slid.

Anton left his body. The window was open, the screen loose, and he was yelling while hanging half out of the yellow house before he was able to stop the body he was no longer controlling. Delilah wasn't answering him. Oh god, was she dead? Wait, no. She was moving. She was answering. She sounded embarrassed, annoyed, in pain. Her voice was huskier than he thought it should be. Was she trying not to cry? She was bleeding, she was shaking. Anton needed to go down and help her.

No, he didn't. He needed to stay far away. But damn, she needed *someone* to help her. Someone needed to protect her from herself. Anton pulled his head inside, fetched the handyman's card from his desk, and threw it to the girl in the driveway. There, he'd done what he could. And now Delilah sounded angry. Did she just tell him to piss off? Anton was laughing at a beautiful woman telling him to piss off; this was dangerous. He went to the kitchen and brewed a fresh pot of coffee. Drinking it, he found himself back in his body. Back in Elba.

He avoided the window all weekend once he saw the sheriff pick her up, and he didn't see Delilah when he was out running. He doubted she would be capable of running for a while, with the state of her shinbone and what looked like a broken ass. The boyfriend had showed up (speaking of asses) and then left again right away. No-good bastard. Anton didn't understand what Delilah saw in that guy.

On Monday morning Anton found a paper bag of freshly cut Swiss chard on the floor of his deck. It looked like she'd shoved it between the rails. She must have held it over her head and stood on her tiptoes to reach. That would have hurt. Anton shouldn't accept the gift. He wasn't supposed to fraternize or familiarize or something with the natives, the marshal said. But fresh Swiss chard! Anton could make a pesto to die for with Swiss chard.

He put the bag in the refrigerator, and went for his run. Later, opening the garage to get his car out for the monthly mainland trip, he was made to pay for the gift.

'Hi,' Delilah said.

Anton turned, startled. He'd no idea how she'd snuck up on him in the graveled driveway, but then saw she was on her grass verge and she was barefoot. Her knees, as well as her hands, were muddy. She'd been weeding.

'Hi,' she said again. 'I left you some greens in thanks—'

'Yeah, thanks. I found them.' Anton forced himself to speak so she would stop. Her husky voice slayed him. He was pleased he had remembered the tone correctly. He wasn't completely mad yet.

'I called that handyman,' she said, brushing the drying dirt off her hands. 'He's coming out soon.'

Anton didn't know how to respond so he finished opening the garage door. He worried that he was staring at her. He removed the chain from the post on his side of the driveway.

'About that chain,' Delilah said.

Anton stopped and turned. She stopped talking, looked him in the eyes, and put her hands in her pockets. One hand was still bandaged. The pause was lasting too long, the eye contact as well. Anton couldn't move away.

'Is it really necessary?' she finished asking with a half shrug.

'Yes,' he said. 'It is.'

She sighed. He sighed in response.

'Look,' he said, and she laughed.

He raised an eyebrow (*What was funny?*) and started over.

'You've never seen what these tourists are like in the height of summer. They're like locusts. They're everywhere. They block the driveway, block the garage, drop trash. They are awful.'

Delilah started to smile. He hurried to stop his own from forming. A glimpse of her one crooked eyetooth would be his downfall.

'They drop trash *everywhere*,' he said. 'What if they got in your garden, huh? How'd you like people stomping through the vegetables, dropping trash?'

She stopped smiling and her eyes widened. She glanced over her shoulder into her garden, anxious now. The squash vines were climbing up the corn stalks, the giant sunflowers were not yet giant but showed promise, and the marigolds edging the beds were riotous bangs of color as they bloomed their heads off. 'Okay,' she said.

'The chain stays.'

Anton nodded and dropped the end of the chain that he'd been holding tightly. She stepped forward, onto the gravel, closer to him. As her bare feet sank into the tiny stones, she winced.

'My name's Delilah,' she said. 'What's yours?'

Anton felt light-headed. He took a few steps toward the safety of his car. The unpaved garage smelled like gasoline, mildew, and loneliness. She was waiting for his answer.

'My name is Anton.'

'Really?'

'No,' he said, and immediately thought, *Oh my god.*

'Really?!'

'Do you even have a sense of humor?' He sounded like a jerk, but she was laughing.

'Go on,' she said, waving him to his car. She picked up the chain from the gravel. 'I'll close it behind you.'

Anton fled. He got in the car that wasn't his, drove it to the ferry, crossed the water, and met with the marshal who, unfortunately, was his. He was out of his body again. Anton was not accustomed to the sensation. Maybe he never would be, but he was beginning to enjoy it. For the first time in his two years and four months of exile, Anton couldn't wait to get back to Elba. He'd worry about that later.

To Espalier an Apple

After the handyman, Roy, finished digging out every second sandstone slab from the backyard, moved them to the front garden path, and smoothed the holes, he went away. Delilah had circled him like a feral cat meeting another cat in her particular alley the entire time he'd been on the property. Her hands clenched and unclenched when Roy handled her wheelbarrow, as if physically stopping herself from jerking it away. He'd brought his own shovel and crowbar, removing them from his small red truck which he'd backed up the graveled drive, Delilah opening and closing the driveway chain for him. Anton watched from above as Roy arrived and departed. Each time the chain clinked into place his head nodded in satisfaction. More tourists arrived on the island every day.

Roy was almost completely silent and worked with an economy of movement. He was probably in his thirties, wore a thin wedding band, and never once looked Delilah in the eye. She felt powerful, like a Gorgon. Roy accepted the cash she handed him with a muffled thanks and quickly drove away. Delilah ran back to the garden, grabbed a shovel, and reclaimed her land.

The next week she spent on her knees planting herbs she'd ordered from Island Hardware. She'd argued with Maisie Thompson over every single herb, but good-naturedly almost. Maisie didn't seem to know how to interact without arguing, and Delilah found Maisie's personal antipathy to thyme entertaining. '—It stinks something awful,' Maisie ended. 'But if you want a stinky garden that's your business.'

Delilah carefully separated the tender roots of the new herbs into smaller sections that she placed into holes she scooped with her fingers in the freshly spaded and amended soil. She planted in the mornings after her run. Sometimes she drank from the garden hose, still sweaty from her exertion, so unwilling was she to waste time entering the house for a glass. In the afternoons, she walked around the garden, plotting. In the evenings, she rode her bike to Ted's to report on each day's progress.

When Alan drove up that Friday, the foreign

car's tires crunching on the gravel, she raised a dazed face to his greeting. She was in her overalls, on her knees, black earth under her nails and up to her elbows. She spared a thought that he hadn't bothered to close the chain behind his car. The driveway was exposed.

'Hi,' Alan said again, his tone impatient. 'I'm here.'

For a full thirty seconds there was no sign she recognized Alan at all, let alone welcomed him. Then knowledge flooded her. This was Alan. He held expectations. Delilah had obligations. Her work-reddened cheeks flushed deeper as she scrambled to her feet. He avoided her muddy embrace, looking equally flustered. They retired, without speaking, into the house.

Inside the kitchen, Alan stood in the doorway leading to the enclosed stairs. He had to duck to walk up them and he looked as if he were preparing to do so as he leaned there, head drooping to regard his tasseled loafers. Delilah left her boots on the porch, dropped her filthy overalls into the washing machine, and washed her hands at the sink. She scrubbed under each nail with the snail-shaped brush. Her long-sleeved thermal undershirt was her only garment, but Alan didn't even raise his head.

'Let's get out of here,' he said.

'What?'

'I said,' he raised his face to look at hers. 'Let's get out of here.'

Delilah's wet hands dripped on the floor. The drops splashed her feet so she grabbed a towel and dried them before squatting to wipe up the floor. She threw the towel into the machine with her overalls.

'Let's go out to dinner in the city. Let's go home,' Alan said when she didn't immediately agree. 'Spend the night. Maybe see a film. When is the last time we went out?'

Never. Delilah thought. *That would be never. You don't want to run into your friends, your family, or especially your wife. We've never gone out.* She remained silent.

'Put your city clothes on, baby,' Alan said, seemingly encouraged by her lack of response. 'Pack a bag, let's go.'

Delilah finally moved. She nodded in acknowledgment; she did not smile. She walked toward the stairs, but he stepped away quickly, thinking she meant to embrace him. She was so grubby.

'Take your time, baby,' Alan said. 'Have a bath. I'll make sure the place is locked up, maybe rest my eyes.'

Without a word or gesture Delilah disappeared upstairs. She bathed; she dressed. She made up her face, then she packed a small bag before waking Alan from his deep slumber on the gold-painted bed. Walking outside, he chatted about options of places in which to eat, see a show, and get a room. He put forth places in the city no one he knew ever frequented. He never noticed that Delilah hadn't said a word. She didn't look up at the yellow house as she left the cottage. Alan didn't realize Delilah wasn't speaking, but then neither did Delilah.

She held the small overnight bag as she walked awkwardly in her high-heeled sandals through the gravel to ride shot-gun in Alan's car. He hadn't put the car into the garage, so eager was he to remove her to neutral territory.

On Monday morning Delilah took the first ferry, arriving home alone on the island. Her city shoes were not meant for long walks, so she kicked them off once she disembarked the ferry. Ted found her this way, barefoot and carrying an overnight bag. He drove her to the cottage in his cruiser. She climbed into the vehicle with only a wry wink as a greeting. At the shared driveway, as she stood in the gravel connecting her home to the yellow house, she only remembered to thank Ted when he'd started to drive away, arm hanging from his open window.

'See you later?' she asked in addition, tentative

for the first time in their relationship.

'Of course.' Ted waved goodbye, his arm no longer hanging forlornly.

Upstairs in the yellow house a window banged shut. Ted drove off when Delilah was safely inside the cottage. They never talked about this later. It was like the morning walk and silent drive never took place.

Delilah finished the herb garden in record time, fearing more interruptions. Planted, mulched, and gently watered, it was beautiful. In six months, when the greenery filled in the bare spots to overlap the soft beige sandstone, it would be prettier still. Delilah took a photo of what she had done and then stood motionless, feeling forlorn. She looked up, beyond the herbs and the sandstone, and the delicate green wrought-iron table and chairs, to the willows that covered the fence. She saw that the willows were sad, raggedy excuses for trees, and Delilah realized that they had to go.

She was still standing there, staring, filing through various tree options in her mind, when Anton finished his run. He came up the beach path loose and relaxed from the exertion, but paused when he spied her. The camera disturbed him until he understood the herb garden was finished and she was recording her achievement. Anton remembered photographing the first successful cheesecake he'd ever produced, and found his feet moving toward Delilah.

Hearing the crunch of the gravel, Delilah woke from her reverie. She didn't turn to look at him, but pointed into the garden.

'Thanks for Roy,' she said. 'Look.'

'Looks nice.' Anton was sincere, although 'nice' was too tame a word. The herb garden was elegant and charming, a perfect spot for morning tea or an evening glass of wine, but Anton was afraid of becoming too honest with her. To maintain distance, he mentally added an outdoor patio to his imaginary restaurant, the game that he hadn't needed to play since Delilah's arrival. But the couple enjoying their glasses of wine while sharing a cannoli were looking a little too familiar and Anton jerked his mind back to Delilah's garden, away from his fantasy. He took a step back, away from her. He couldn't risk being so close to her. He was afraid to be his true self. The self who wasn't Anton.

'Roy did a good job, although I think I scared him.' She didn't seem concerned.

'His name is Ray,' Anton said. *Hadn't she read the card?*

'He said Roy.'

'No, he said Ray because that's his name, and you misheard.'

'Is everyone on this island lying about their name?' Delilah asked. She was staring into the rough willows at the fence line.

'Why?' Anton's attention was caught. 'What's your real name?'

'Dolores,' Delilah said. 'Can you imagine? I'm named for my grandmother, my *abuela*. I changed it as soon as I could.'

'You do look like a Dolores,' Anton said.

She jerked her head to stare at him, not liking his statement. He was studying her closely, like he'd just met her. Or like he'd had a head injury. She grimaced at him.

'I do not,' she said. 'Stop it. And don't tell anyone.'

Anton laughed an abrupt snort. 'Who would I tell? I don't talk to anyone.'

'Don't tell Alan,' Delilah said. 'Or…'

'Huh.' Anton started to walk away. 'I don't even know who that is.'

Delilah was left standing in the driveway, her mouth half open.

'The garden looks nice,' Anton said again, almost at his deck. He spoke to her over his shoulder. 'See you around, Dolores.'

He heard a sharp thunk, like she'd kicked a stone, but when he turned at the top of his deck stairs, she'd gone.

Ted came in to see the garden, a bit nervous because Delilah had waved him in when he'd been driving by in the cruiser. He was on duty, but he couldn't resist her smile or the enthusiastic gesture of her beckoning arm. He was worried lines were being blurred. Maybe he should have worried about that sooner. He wondered who was watching as the sound of the gravel crunching under the cruiser's tires made him cringe.

All watching eyes were forgotten when Delilah took him by the hand to drag him to the area behind the cottage. She wanted him to see what she had made. His wife's ill health had prevented them from having children, but Ted always wanted to be a father. In the current situation this thought made Ted extremely uncomfortable and he banished it. He was glad he did when, once behind the screen of the cottage, Delilah threw her arms around his neck and kissed him in a less than daughterly way.

When she pulled back, her eyes were looking over his shoulder. The back of his neck tingling, Ted turned. There was no one in the driveway.

They were alone.

'The garden is finished, I see,' he said, turning back to it. 'Beautiful job.'

'Yes, it is! Thanks for figuring out the logistics.' She patted him solicitously on the arm. In doing so she bumped her elbow on his service revolver and shied away. 'Now, turn your mind to this problem.'

She pointed to the willows, and then opened her palm in a questioning, almost exasperated, gesture.

'What? The trees?' he asked. He walked closer to where the trees obscured the fence. He reached through the tangled branches, pushing them aside, and thumped the wooden fence behind them.

'The trees aren't hurting the fence,' he said, and Delilah frowned. He grinned at her. 'They aren't hurting the fence because it's cedar. Mr. Oakapple next door believed in building to last.'

Delilah was entirely uninterested in the neighbors on the side with whom she did not share a driveway and her face reflected this. She wanted to be rid of the ugly, tangled willows, but she also believed in preserving trees wherever possible. She wanted Ted to solve her problem for her. She tilted her head and gave him the look that always worked, no matter who the man. The trick to the look was to imagine what you would do to reward the man should he please you—and keep the image in your thoughts as you held his gaze. Depending on the intuition of the man, and the vividness of his imagination, this look worked within seconds to minutes. It worked now.

'Cedar is pretty, too,' Ted said, flushing and shifting his stance. He moved back to her side to take her hand. 'Without the willows you'd see the red wood.'

Delilah smiled encouragingly and gently patted his hand before drifting away. Ted moved with her. Even distracted, the couple stepped carefully to avoid the delicate herbs settling in the soil.

'Cedar is wonderful for espaliering,' Ted said, still seeking her. 'It is an herb garden. You could espalier a fruit tree to the fence. I have apple trees!'

Delilah saw the idea seed in his mind's eye. He dropped her gaze in order to turn and study the fence, the willows, the amount of sunlight reaching them. She saw his gardening instinct win out over lust. She hugged her arms around her waist. She loved older men.

'I have two baby apple trees I grew from seed,' Ted continued, pacing off the fence line. He was stepping carefully, one foot in front of the other, on the stones. 'Have you ever espaliered a tree?'

Delilah shook her head. She smiled again, a satisfied smile now, verging on triumphant, and sat down on the steps of the cottage. She lifted her face to the sun. 'Tell me about it,' she said.

The morning after Anton watched Delilah kissing the sheriff (and what was *that* about?) he finished his run at the same moment that Delilah, coming from the opposite direction, finished hers. They didn't speak. Delilah jerked her head sideways before heading down the path, expecting him to follow. Anton did. Not only did he live down the path anyway, but she had a look on her face that... what? He asked himself, *What about her face?*

Anton wanted to know what she wanted from him, it was as simple as that. But nothing in life is ever as simple as that. Delilah was filling two glasses from a pitcher of water on her wrought-iron table. The pitcher was made of ceramic, marbled pink with a large blue rose. It reminded Anton of something his nonna might have used. The glasses were regular juice glasses, but she'd put a lace doily on the tray. Clearly she'd planned this visit.

She took her glass and sat on the porch steps

where she picked up a waiting coffee-table book. Anton tried to resent that he'd been set up as he grabbed the glass meant for him and joined her on the steps. She patted the soft wooden top step next to her and, God help him, all Anton felt was pleased.

Delilah placed the book on his lap. He drained the water from his glass before handing it to her. She gave it a glance before setting it behind her. Anton understood that she wasn't going to wait on him. He grinned.

She ignored his high spirits and flipped open the book to a marked page. She pointed.

'Look,' she said. She sounded horrified.

The page read: 'To Espalier an Apple', and it gave step-by-step instructions next to detailed photographs. Anton studied the page, then flipped to the next one. Delilah averted her eyes to focus on the willow trees.

'The willows are ugly,' Delilah said. 'I want them gone, but...'

'You can't bring yourself to crucify an apple tree?' Anton winced at the photograph depicting a hole being drilled through a slender branch in order to anchor it to the wired fence behind it.

'I guess it looks elegant when it's done and all'—Delilah turned the page to examine the final photograph—'but I don't think I can do it. I can't split and cut and drill baby branches and screw them to a fence.'

'I take it someone else thinks you should?'

Delilah nodded. She pulled the rubber band from her hair and let the black curtain fall down to obscure her face from his view.

'So don't do it,' Anton said, closing the book. He handed it back to her. 'It's your garden, your call.'

'What do you do in there?' she asked him. 'What do you do all day?'

Anton, caught unaware, heard himself responding. He heard his voice from a great distance.

'I'm writing a book,' his voice said. 'A memoir, not a cookbook. And I'm planning my restaurant.'

'Why isn't it a cookbook?' Delilah must have been interested because she pushed her hair back in order to study his face.

'Because...' *Stop talking*, he thought. 'Because it's a memoir.'

'Oh, I see,' Delilah said. 'What's your real name?'

Then Anton's self-preservation kicked in or muscle memory or just common sense. *Why would she ask that?* He stopped talking, giving up information, but he couldn't stop staring at her. She was sitting so close. Her black hair was curling in sweaty wisps at her temples, her earlobe was pierced but empty, and her cacao-colored irises stared back at him, bemused. *What harm would it do to tell her the truth?*

Here was a conundrum, though. Was Anton the one thinking this? Or was it Delilah? Maybe telling her the truth would do a lot of harm, maybe none at all. Anton was beginning to lose sight of his boundaries, his goals. He summoned a picture of his marshal's long-suffering face at their last meeting, which didn't help much. Anton pictured his nonna disappointed in him when his manicotti dissolved into an inedible mess. This snapped him right out of his enthrallment. Delilah was waiting. Let her wait.

She flipped the black hair aside to look at him. He wiped the sweat off his brow with the back of one hand. She was still looking at him. He was thirsty and obviously she wasn't going to offer him another glass of water. He reached behind her to snag his glass. She didn't move and he was forced to lean in much closer to her body than he'd meant to. She inhaled before delicately releasing her breath in a soft sigh. She hadn't stopped looking at him.

Anton grabbed the glass, his face mere inches from Delilah's, and stood up. He poured water from the curved glass pitcher and drained it from the glass without pausing for breath. Her silence was adding to his discomfort.

'Have you checked the chain this morning?' he asked her and she shook her head. He started around the cottage. 'You have to be diligent or they will get in.'

Walking away to check the chain gave him a chance to calm down and break the lock she had on him with her stare. The chain was there, still in place; everything was fine. Anton did need to break her stare, didn't he? He held two goals on this island: keep the tourists out of his driveway and do not get involved with the locals.

Delilah, though, wasn't really a local. She didn't even want to nail a tree to a fence. She had an *abuela*; she lied about her name. She didn't belong here any more than he did. And she smelled like salty vanilla. Anton started walking back. Maybe she'd like to stare at him some more. Anton thought he'd sensed certain promise in that stare.

When he went around the corner of the cottage, however, the steps were empty. The pitcher and water glasses were gone. The book on how to espalier an apple tree lay abandoned on the top step, its pages ruffling in the bite of the sea breeze that rampaged over the dunes and up the driveway between their separate buildings. Anton went home. He was filled with a sudden desire to make cheesecake. Vanilla cheesecake. He'd put burnt sugar on top.

The Path at the End
of the Driveway

Summer cracked open and the ferry poured forth its river of tourists. They came by foot and car, filling every available hotel room and rentable edifice. The Bradshaws further down Mulberry Street parked their car at the curb, shoved a set of bunkbeds in the garage and made enough money to pay for a new bathroom, but most islanders found that crass. Ray Ramirez told Ted all about it. The Bradshaws hired him to put in the framework for the new ceiling. They were paying Ray under the table because they hadn't bothered to get the proper permits. People were forever telling Ted things he'd just as soon not know.

Ted was so busy patrolling, citing, settling ticket disputes, and answering self-evident questions from wandering visitors that he'd no time for his own personal visitor. His garden was suffering, too. Delilah started going over every other day to do a little work in the neglected space. She was a love of a girl. She left harvested vegetables on his kitchen table along with little notes. Once she left a slightly squashed slice of delicious cheesecake, which surprised him. He hadn't known she baked. She picked the ripe fruit and vegetables, she watered, she brought in his mail and left it in a neat pile by the telephone, but Ted hadn't seen her in days. He missed her.

When the dispatcher radioed in Delilah's address and said she'd called in a trespass complaint, Ted was actually looking forward to seeing her, even if it was in his official capacity. He'd take her in any capacity he could. Delilah was pacing at the mouth of her driveway, her cheeks an agitated red. She wasn't wearing overalls, but a pair of cut-off jeans and a skimpy camisole top.

Delilah's upper lip was beaded with moisture from the heat. She wiped it off with the back of her hand while she explained to Ted why she was upset. Her black hair was not in its usual pony-tail, but was loose. It had grown longer. Ted real-ized she'd never cut it since moving in. Her hair reached almost to her waist. He reached out to touch it where it lay against her back, but stopped his hand. He was on duty.

'They must have undone the chain, see? It was here on the ground when I came home,' Delilah was saying. The chain was back in place, but the damage was done. Two cars were parked in the graveled drive, one blocking the garage of the yellow house. 'Anton is going to be so upset. He always says tourists are like locusts.'

Ted didn't quite follow the last sentence, and he wasn't sure how he felt about Delilah quoting what her neighbor 'always says'. Since when did she even know his name?

'How long have they been here?' Ted finally gave in and touched her, running one hand down her arm. He told himself he did it in order to gain her attention. She hadn't stopped pacing.

'I don't know. After ten?' She shrugged. 'I've been at your place, watering and then I stopped to trade vegetables for eggs from Maisie Thompson —big mistake because the store was packed—and then I got here and the chain was torn down and cars parked. Do you think you can have them towed before Anton gets home? He will be so angry they've blocked his garage.'

'Towed?' Ted was startled. 'Usually I just hunt down the owners and ask them...'

'There's no time for that,' Delilah said, grabbing his hand. 'And really, these people need to be taught a lesson.'

Ted, having never seen this side of Delilah's personality, was experiencing a moment of surrealness. She was a territorial person. He was not allowed in her house because another man paid for it. Fine, he understood that. (He was beginning to hate the other man and plot means of removing him from Delilah's life, but that was a thought for another day.) However, Delilah wasn't upset because she'd come home to tourists trespassing and leaving their cars on her property. She was angry and territorial on behalf of a neighbor who Ted hadn't known she even talked to.

Damn straight Ted was going to have the tourists' cars towed. Then he was going to find the tourists and cite them for trespassing. He hoped they were the loud entitled types who tried to intimidate and throw their weight around because Ted would welcome an excuse to react in a hostile, aggressive manner. Ted was feeling very agitated.

Delilah must have sensed this because she stopped pacing, gave him the once-over, and then looked satisfied. 'Do you want to come in and use my telephone?'

'No, I'll radio from the cruiser.' Ted shot a glare of pure venom at the Camaro blocking the yellow house's garage.

Delilah caught him by surprise then. She stepped up, pressed against him with her arms around his neck and slid her tongue into his mouth. It was bright afternoon, full public, and he was on duty. She moved away, nonchalant as anything, walking over to her front porch to sit on the steps. Ted retreated to his car.

Ted was born and raised on the island. He had only ever gone away to attend the police academy. He returned and married his wife, but even before burying her he'd had only two interests: his work and his garden. Geraldine was a socially expected accompaniment to his life and he'd always assumed that he loved her. They were both disappointed when they didn't have children. They were sad when she got cancer. Ted was even sadder when she died. But Ted realized he couldn't remember her face now, and the love he'd felt for Geraldine was a pale flame in comparison to the blue-white heat of his passion for Delilah.

Before the onslaught of the tourists, the last time he and Delilah were together, Ted, prostrate in his torn-apart bed, thought he might be having a heart attack. The muscle was beating in a syncopated rhythm similar to the noise his old Bronco made right before its carburetor gave out. He was unable to catch his breath. Delilah was sipping water, looking sleepy.

'I think you might be the death of me,' Ted said when he could speak. Delilah put down her glass of water in order to face him. 'I wouldn't mind... Death by Delilah would be worth it.' Ted's heartbeat settled into a calmer pace.

Delilah laughed. She looked fully awake now, sleepiness banished by what, exactly, Ted couldn't imagine. Worry for Ted's imminent doom? Pleasure in his compliment? Pride in having him completely at her mercy? Sheriff Ted held no desire to know the thoughts of his citizenry; he knew it was for the best that every man and woman was their own island, here on the island (Ted smiled), but occasionally he wished that he understood Delilah just a little.

She was looking at him as he thought this, face-to-face, as she'd settled in close on her right side to study him. Her large, black-fringed eyes—there was a black ring around the brown iris that gave them a depth so that Ted understood the hackneyed phrase 'drowning in her eyes' for the first time—were locked on his. He had absolutely no idea what she was thinking. He wouldn't even attempt a guess.

'Death by Delilah,' he said again.

She smiled, lowered her eyes, and leaned in. He thought she meant to kiss him. At the last moment she swooped lower and bit him on the shoulder. It was not a love bite, she sank her teeth in hard enough that he carried the red mark the rest of the day. The next morning, the red mark was a dark-blue, half-moon bruise.

Even the bruise made him happy.

Now, bruise gone as if it had never existed, it had been so long since they'd been together (another reason the sheriff had less patience with the tourists' shenanigans), and making his way toward the path at the end of Delilah's driveway, Ted remembered Delilah's latest garden improvement. He paused to regard the newly exposed fence behind the herb garden. He thought of it as his own mark upon her property. Admiring Delilah's obsessive gardening habits, Ted fully expected to see the two little apple trees he'd given her neatly espaliered to the pinky-red cedar. He did not see this. His pause lengthened.

The apple trees were neatly planted all right. They looked bright and healthy, no sign of shock. Both trees had correct basins of soil around them, drip lines placed carefully under the smooth layer of mulch. But they weren't espaliered; they held their original bushy forms and stood out from the fence a good three feet. Ted felt pulled in multiple directions, but the honk of the arriving tow-truck's horn decided him. He wondered how long, exactly, he had been standing in Delilah's garden, staring at the baby apple trees.

He turned around to deal with the tow-truck driver. He was still dealing with the driver when a sunburnt tourist wearing a stupid hat like Gilligan came tearing down the graveled drive. This gentleman was not the owner of the garage-blocking Camaro, but the driver of the rented Ford station wagon. Ted felt bad towing the car of a guy who not only had a mean-looking wife and three puny children, but also terrible taste in hats, so Ted didn't tow his rental car. He did, however, give him a citation with the maximum fine available and a stern warning about trespassing and vandalism.

The mean-looking wife—Ted wasn't sure what exactly about her made him uncomfortable but he recognized 'mean' when he saw it—wanted to protest his allegation.

'Why do you say "vandalism"?' The woman's face was sunburnt as well as sour. She pushed past her husband, the children scattering and then re-assembling in the farthest end of the Ford. They watched from the safety of the open window.

Then Delilah was at her gate. Until the wife got involved Delilah seemed content to oversee the proceedings from her porch steps. Ted knew she was there, of course, but was trying to ignore her. She was drinking lemonade. But when the wife walked forward, Delilah put down her glass and moved closer, silently yet somehow obtrusively.

Delilah didn't need to speak; she just leaned against the wooden post. She'd washed her face, combed her hair, but she still wore the skimpy top and cut-off jeans. There was no visible reason for her to make anyone nervous. She stood with her weight on one leg, hip thrust out. She rubbed her left hand over her exposed right collarbone and slowly moved her gaze over the wife. The other woman, wind-blown, bedraggled with beach sand and child-rearing, over forty and overweight, flushed even redder than her sunburn.

'Pulling down a chain marked private property, throwing it in the dirt and driving over it,' Ted said again slowly. 'Vandalism and trespassing.'

The wife and Delilah were still eyeing each other in a manner Ted didn't even want to understand. Whatever passed between them—a strange expression almost like gloating was on Delilah's face—caused the wife to abruptly turn around and climb into the passenger seat of the Ford.

'Let's go, Jimmy,' was all she said.

Jimmy took the ticket from Ted and got behind the wheel. He backed the long car out of the driveway onto Mulberry Street. Jimmy and his wife never met Ted's eyes again, but from the farthest end of the car the smallest child waved bye-bye. Ted waved back before securing the driveway chain.

When he turned around Delilah was back on the steps. Her glass was empty. As Ted walked over he told himself he'd handled this as he would have any trespassing complaint. *Perfectly normal*, he thought.

'I have tonight off,' he said, ruining normality.

'It's Friday,' Delilah said. She opened her hands apologetically.

'Have you ever thought—' Ted said. When his radio crackled from the cruiser cutting off his sentence, Delilah was not the only one relieved.

He had to go, and he walked to his cruiser. 'Monday,' he called over his shoulder. It wasn't a question, and he couldn't see her face.

'Thank you, Sheriff,' Delilah said loudly in response. When he faced her again in order to enter the cruiser, she waved bye-bye exactly like the departing child.

Ted left to help with a drunk-and-disorderly call on the other side of the island. He didn't see Delilah again until Monday. By then he'd forgotten all about the apple trees that she hadn't espaliered. He had more important things on his mind.

The Iris Walk

On an island overrun by tourists it became necessary to rise earlier in order to run before the beach was clogged with human detritus and other hazards of a life lived in hiding. Anton started running when the light was still pearly and the world damp. Occasionally he saw Delilah setting out as he was coming in. Even sleepy-eyed and bed-headed she was so tempting he looked away and mentally catalogued the ingredients of a roux—the least sexy recipe he could think of.

The light lasted so long in the summer, the sunlight lingering in a strange dusk for hours it seemed, that Anton was able to see the gravel churned and furrowed in the driveway, and the little metal sign hanging crookedly on its chain when he came home that evening. He'd been shopping on the mainland and hadn't paid attention to the time.

He put the car in the garage and was standing in the gloom trying to read the story written in the driveway's gravel when he realized Delilah was standing outside, too. She was further up the drive, next to her back porch, but there was light in the upstairs of her cottage and music playing. She was waving Anton closer, beckoning to him, with her lover in the house. Anton knew his marshal would want him to turn around and use the front door of the yellow house or leap in the car and make the last ferry back to the mainland and safety.

Safety from familiarity and involvement and beckoning gestures from beautiful neighbors he'd found seductive before she'd laughed at his rude jokes, or given him chard, or spoken to him with that cat's-tongue voice. Now she was standing in the shadows of approaching dark with her rich boyfriend overhead listening to *Don Giovanni* (*what a poser*) and she was enticing Anton toward her. He should run the other way. He walked briskly across the disturbed driveway. Delilah took hold of his sleeve and pulled him closer.

'You were right,' she whispered into his ear, and Anton knew he'd been waiting his entire life for someone to tell him this. 'They are locusts.'

Oh, tourists. His heart left his mouth and settled in his chest once more. She had met the tourists and realized they were the enemy.

'They broke in when I was at the hardware.' She was still whispering. 'I called the sheriff, and had one car towed and another ticketed.'

She leaned back in order to see his face, await a response, but at the same time she released her grip of his short sleeve and slid her hand down his bicep and forearm to take his hand. He wasn't able to speak. He understood she'd probably lost her balance in the gravel and needed assistance in the dark or, being so goofy, didn't even know she was touching her neighbor. She, sweet-scented from her bath and he, who hadn't been touched in any but the most casual way—hello, nice to meet you, here's your change or your dry cleaning—in over two years. When he felt the rough skin of her palm, as sandpapery as her husky voice, he was rendered mute by desire.

She didn't mind, or maybe she didn't notice, because she kept speaking even as his fingers clutched hers and his palm snuggled closer. His other hand, having reflexively dropped the bag of groceries, covered the back and wrist of both her hands. They stood, sinking in gravel, ankle deep in spilled groceries, all hands touching, his head dipped low to hear her soft words. The bats were dark ellipses overhead.

'The woman tried to argue about the vandalism, but the sign is bent and luckily Ted was cranky because I didn't espalier the apple trees he gave me.' She gestured with her head toward the back garden. 'Remember?'

Inside, Don Giovanni stopped bellowing and Delilah jumped in the sudden silence. Anton tightened his grip on her hands. He was afraid she would pull away.

'Anyway, that's why the gravel is a mess. I didn't want you to worry. Goodnight.' She pulled her hands from his and darted away (her injury must have been healing nicely), but before she left him standing in the now full dark, between 'worry' and 'goodnight,' she stood on tiptoe and kissed his cheek. It wasn't a feathery caress, the type that later he could posit he'd only imagined; it was a loud smack. It was the kind of kiss that comic books displayed with a 'mwah' sound bubble when a heroine bestowed it on her brother or father or a small street urchin. It was the type of kiss, Anton felt, that was worse than no kiss at all.

It distracted him so that he only knew Delilah was gone when the screen door softly shut behind her and the kitchen light was extinguished, leaving Anton to find his spilled groceries and bag them by feel before blindly walking to his deck stairs more from memory than any physical sense. Anton was left with the belief that Delilah knew exactly what she was doing with that parting kiss, and that lead to other beliefs and thoughts, the kind of thoughts that kept him awake at night.

Thoughts about Delilah and the boyfriend; Delilah and himself; Delilah and the tourists; Delilah and the smacking kiss; and thoughts about Delilah and the sheriff. For no discernable reason, here is where Anton drew the line. He couldn't think about Delilah and the sheriff. He wouldn't.

The sheriff was someone Anton was not going to think about ever again. Although he had to admit to himself, not to Delilah—to her Anton admitted nothing because speaking with her after the hand-holding and the kiss was nothing but dangerous—the sheriff didn't bother him in the way horrible Alan bothered him. Anton's current favorite fantasy (okay, second favorite) involved Alan's head and a cafeteria-sized vat of hot marinara—but Anton appreciated the sheriff and Delilah dealing with those locusts.

The next dawn when he spied her finishing her run, he smiled at her. He smiled a wide, friendly smile.

And she followed him home.

Delilah saw a photograph in one of Ted's coffee-table gardening books. She borrowed the book although it made her bicycle lopsided with its unwieldly weight listing her decrepit raffia basket to one side the entire ride home. Her garden was nearing completion and she needed inspiration. The photograph inspired her. Therefore, she took the book. Once home, bike put away, she poured a glass of sumac lemonade and sat on her porch swing and prepared to be further inspired.

The picture of purple fields widened her eyes. It was taken of a lavender farm in France and was so gorgeous—purple fields and little stone walls and olive trees gorgeous—that Delilah wanted to weep with jealousy. She didn't even like lavender, or, at least, the smell of it. It gave her a headache and made the back of her mouth taste like soap, but Delilah wanted a field of beautiful purple. Anything purple. Anything except smelly lavender.

She turned a few pages and there was a close-up of a blooming iris, such a deep rich purple that Delilah's eyes ached in their sockets. Delilah developed a plan. She couldn't have a field of purple and she didn't want lavender, but she could line her driveway with purple iris and it would be stunning. It would be a column of rich color lining the driveway all the way to where the seagrass started, and it wouldn't leave a nasty lavender-soap taste in her mouth or smell like someone's Great Aunt Gisela. Delilah reached into the basket next to the porch swing that contained all the catalogues she'd taken from Ted's house. She had to hunt down the perfect purple available in her zone, and sized for the space.

She paid for express shipping when she ordered the irises; she didn't want to wait any longer than necessary. Lately Delilah felt antsy, anxious. She felt like she was waiting but she didn't know for what. Even 'waiting' wasn't the right word. Delilah felt a craving, like she needed something delicious to eat, but she couldn't decide what that might be. Not sweet, not salty, not that other one she could never remember. It wasn't thirst—she wanted to bite something. It wasn't Alan or Ted; she'd tried that. Biting them didn't satisfy Delilah, but she felt she was closer to the truth.

Delilah was worried she knew deep down who she wanted to bite. She knew what she was craving, but admitting that would change everything, for everyone. She wasn't ready to face that yet so she was going to plant a long narrow bed of iris so purple it'd make a viewer's eyes ache. Maybe that would tide Delilah's dissatisfaction over. If only for a while.

On Monday, she tried to explain her new iris project to Ted, but for the first time he wasn't interested in garden plans. Oh, he listened, or at least waited patiently while Delilah spoke from her usual spot at his kitchen table, mint tea warming her hands. Ted was crafting grilled cheese sandwiches at his stove.

'It would draw the eye up and out, you see.' Delilah used spoons and a butter knife to represent her driveway. 'Draw the eye away from the garage—so ugly. You'd only see the column of purple.'

The cut-glass napkin holder became the house on the other side of her driveway and she stopped talking. Ted placed her plated lunch on her model vegetable garden, over lace placemats his wife had dyed lime green, and the utensil driveway disintegrated as Delilah used the knife to cut her sandwich and Ted stirred his coffee with a spoon.

'You have options,' Ted said. Delilah froze with her knife in the air. She carefully put it down on the plate. It nestled on the ridged edge of the green Fiestaware.

'Like lavender?' Delilah got up and removed the ketchup from the refrigerator. 'Yucky, no thank you. And butterfly bushes are too big. It has to be purple *and* small enough to step over.'

'Not the garden,' Ted said. He took a bite of his sandwich and talked around it. 'I'm not talking about plants.'

Delilah stopped dipping her grilled cheese into the puddle of ketchup on her plate. She glanced up, wary, and then back down. She quickly bit off the red-coated corner of her sandwich before it could drip and chewed it neatly.

'You have other options,' Ted repeated. 'If you want—'

'Well, I am,' Delilah said. She was staring at the napkins in the cut-glass holder. Ted handed her one. 'I am talking about the garden.'

It was Ted's turn to be wary. He'd never heard that tone from her, so firm, so assertive. She was talking about her garden, the tone implied, and only her garden. She was meticulously wiping her fingers with the napkin, scrubbing the nail bed and between each finger. She frowned with concentration.

'All right,' Ted said, and he stopped eating. 'All right, tell me again about the lavender.'

'*Not* lavender,' she responded instantly. 'Anything but lavender. I ordered irises.'

She smiled at him finally, but there was something in that smile. A little hesitant? No, distant. It was the smile she offered to babies and the elderly. It was her public smile. It filled him with trepidation. The sheriff felt all the hair stand up on the back of his neck and he rubbed his arms briskly to get rid of the goosebumps that rose to warn him.

Delilah, hands clean of grilled-cheese grease, flipped open another gardening magazine from the pile of mail on Ted's kitchen table. She needed Ted to stop telling her about options, stop making her offers she'd have to refuse. Why were men born to ruin good things?

In the magazine was a photograph of a cottage next to the ocean. The article was about grasses, tough, sturdy, hardy-growing grasses. Delilah didn't read it. She had no room for grass meadows and anyway her garden was almost done. The photograph of the cottage reminded her of the photograph in the real estate catalogue Alan had brought her over a year ago.

The photograph of her cottage was cropped so that the shared driveway was not shown, the yellow house looming next door was missing. One mostly saw the gray weathered walls, the white-painted shutters and railed porch, and the white picket fence surrounding the autumnal garden. Even through the medium of the blurry catalogue page, Delilah could hear the cottage calling to be saved. It needed to be cleaned and cared for; the garden wanted to be beautiful.

Alan liked the price, the remoteness, the aging community, and Delilah's eagerness. In Alan's mind, her eagerness to possess the cottage was leverage. She wasn't unaware of this fact. Delilah knew there were options. She had always understood her options, and the cost of each one.

Delilah had opted out of her job at the city's botanical garden and her shared flat with other family-less girls once she met Alan and (after a few dates) he had told her about his empty apartment. Once she'd moved into that apartment, Alan had then told her about his wife and family in his house on the other side of the city, but Delilah understood the situation in detail. The apartment Delilah shared with the mostly absent Alan was twice the size and much warmer than the one where she'd shared a bedroom with a girl that Delilah barely knew and had no inclination to ever know better. Without her job Delilah busied herself redecorating the apartment, painting the walls, sewing new curtains, and reupholstering the furniture, but there was nothing like a garden. Walking in the city's parks or the occasional weekend trip to the country didn't satisfy Delilah's needs. By the time she became truly restless, Alan arrived with real estate catalogues and once again Delilah weighed her options.

Alan was the price Delilah paid for her cottage, her garden, her accounts at the grocery and hardware. Alan was the price she was willing to pay; she'd been willing to pay. Now, almost a year later, she didn't want Ted complicating things with his own brand of options. She didn't want Ted to be the price she paid. She didn't want to think of him like that. She didn't want to think about her cost of living.

It was so much better, much more beautiful, more tranquil, *easier,* to think about a line of purple iris leading the viewer off, away from the cottage and the garden and the cost of all that Delilah paid—one way or another. Better to think about beauty.

In her enthusiasm to quench her craving for beauty, she bought too many irises. After two days of dawn-to-dusk work on her knees, digging a trench, adding bone meal and iris rhizomes, and filling the trench in again, she still had irises to spare. She stood slowly, her joints creaking and popping like her old dolls' legs, and she found herself facing the yellow house.

The yellow house had nothing like a garden. In the front grew that lone blue spruce, a misshapen monster that shaded the garage and the front of Anton's house, but that was it. No flowers, no shrubs, not even a scrawny willow or some saw-edged seagrass softened the barrenness of the yellow house's exterior. The gravel of the drive went all the way to the yellow skirting of the house, but surely, Delilah thought, there was enough soil for a line of iris rhizomes? All she would have to do was spade the gravel back, dig another trench, shove the soil and gravel back in, and voila! The purple would look startling against the bitter-yellow wall. Anton wouldn't even have to know.

But, no. Delilah realized that wouldn't be honest of her. Besides, even Anton would notice the flowers when they appeared. He was so territorial, he might be angry she'd gone onto his side of the driveway. He might consider her a locust, too. She'd better talk to him about the joys of purple iris lining both sides of the driveway, the beauty of symmetry. She'd ask him tomorrow after their run; until then, she placed the waiting irises in her detached garage, on the soil floor under the work bench with its dusty shelves containing dark items best forgotten. Rhizomes should always be stored in a cool dark place. Delilah was someone who liked everything, and everyone, in their proper space.

Anton said no. Delilah followed him down the beach path onto his deck. He'd smiled at her after their run, a wide sweet smile. He'd looked delighted to see her, so happy she thought he'd be thrilled for her to follow him. Maybe he'd feed her breakfast. Anton knew about cooking, about food. Maybe he could solve her weird craving.

But then he looked worried on the deck. Even though she'd kicked her shoes off like he did, he still squinted in anxiety when he looked at her. He let her into the kitchen, though, and offered her a glass of water. He listened politely enough to the iris walk idea.

'Just one side of the driveway will look lop-sided, see?' Delilah drew a line with one finger on his floury countertop. Then she added a second line equidistant. 'But two lines of purple iris? Spectacular.'

Anton drank more water, refilling his glass at the tap. She set down her still-full glass in order to elaborate on the diagram of their driveway. Once she added Mulberry Street and wavy lines for the ocean, she picked up the glass of water and drank it. She wiped the back of her hand over her mouth. He was watching her, but silently.

'It'll be so easy,' she said. 'I'm only asking for your blessing. I've got it, right?'

And then he said no. Delilah couldn't believe it. Again she explained the beauty of symmetry, the lustrous glow of purple pulling the eye, the ease of trenching and her willingness to do all the labor. He said no again, offering no further explanation.

'Why not?' Delilah asked him. 'What's wrong with it? What's wrong with you?'

'I think it would be pointless,' Anton said. 'Just, no.' He cocked his head and waited for her response.

In her shock at his obstruction she stared at

him. She stared at him so hard that he shifted uncomfortably where he stood leaning against his sink. Anton had baked the evening before and their bare feet were coated with flour kicked up from the floor. Delilah did not think highly of Anton's housekeeping; her floor would have been swept and mopped by now. Her counters would be squeaky clean. Delilah continued to stare, and Anton looked serious.

She wasn't thinking about rewarding his behavior, but of picking up one of the skinny loaves of long bread that reposed on the racks on the counter and hitting him over the head with it. She was staring hard into his eyes, and no doubt there was a promise there, but she couldn't believe it promised anything good. Why was he thwarting her? Why didn't he agreeably go along with her plans for the driveway? Didn't he realize she only wanted to create beauty?

Delilah's craving to bite was manifesting itself and maybe that is what Anton read in her eyes. Anton acted. He stepped forward and kissed her. He pressed her up against the counter containing the long loaves of bread and kissed her some more. Delilah, forgoing hitting him over the head with a loaf, kissed him back. The iris walk was forgotten, Ted and Alan forgotten, her craving was building and building.

Delilah kissed Anton and Anton kissed

Delilah until they both stopped for air, and then they stared at each other again. Anton smiled finally, a friendly grin like he was saying 'hello'. Delilah, still looking into his eyes, but no longer able to remember what it was, exactly, that she had wanted from him, smiled back. Anton leaned over and kissed her gently on the forehead, the way one kisses a child being tucked into bed.

'Further gardening is pointless because I think we should leave,' Anton said. Delilah scuffed her feet in the flour and tilted her face up to be kissed again. Anton obliged. 'Do you think we should leave?'

'Actually,' Delilah said. She bit him on the collarbone. 'I do. I think we should leave. I've finished my garden.'

'Well then,' Anton said. 'Naturally, you have no reason to stay.'

Delilah was sad for a moment, thinking of Ted, but then Anton, perhaps realizing this, quickly kissed all thoughts of other men away. Conversation was paused until they slipped on the slick, messy floor, separating and laughing. She didn't want to ever stop kissing him.

The Last Ferry

The ferry was late. Alan was forced to sit in line, waiting, breathing in the exhaust from cars whose owners didn't have the decency to cut their engines. This, after he'd left the city, left his house, early, thinking he'd surprise Delilah with a morning arrival. He imagined her delight at seeing him hours and days ahead of schedule. Maybe they'd take a walk on the beach, enjoy the roar of the waves, discuss the new direction their life together was about to take. But the ferry was late because the end-of-summer tourists were unruly and the ferry captain couldn't maintain enough order to depart the island, unload the sunburnt rabble and ready the vessel for the return trip in a timely manner. Alan felt that a tighter ship should be run. He smiled at his own joke.

The line of cars on the causeway began to move and Alan had no further room for reflection until his Porsche was stowed safely, he had a paper cup of tepid coffee in his hand, and a seat out of the spray but with enough breeze to keep comfortable. Alan didn't like to sweat and he had a lot to think about. There were decisions to be made, plans needed forming and steps taken. Alan was accustomed to all that; he welcomed it. But he didn't like ultimatums and Alan had gotten one.

Teresa, Alan's wife, after thirty years of marriage and two kids and two houses and three cars and that stupid horse that no one ever rode, gave Alan an ultimatum. Teresa, it turned out, knew about Delilah. More importantly—in Teresa's exact words—she knew about the cottage Alan had bought for Delilah. Teresa wasn't going to stand for it.

On the top deck of the ferry, in the cooling breeze with a sea spray that only mildly reeked of diesel, Alan's scalp tightened in remembered anxiety. Teresa was willing to put up with a lot; she'd known about Delilah, known about the apartment where Alan paid the rent, and she'd said nothing. Maybe Alan was having a mid-life crisis, she'd said to him the night before. Maybe he needed a fling to settle his nerves or feel like a man again (Alan flinched at this and crossed his legs), but buying this girl young enough to be his daughter a beachfront cottage? Taking the food from his children's mouths in order to feather his love nest?

That Teresa would not tolerate.

Their son was in law school and their daughter was engaged to another lawyer, so Alan didn't think either of them was in danger of losing any meals, but Teresa had that look in her eye that Alan recognized as a warning not to disregard her motherly feelings and he didn't back-talk. He listened quietly to his wife's ultimatum and then slept in the guest room for the rest of the night. At dawn, he'd dressed, walked to the garage where he kept the Porsche and hit the road. Being stymied by the late ferry was unfortunate, but it gave him time to mull.

Two children ran across the deck, a little girl chased by a smaller boy. Right at Alan's feet the girl hit the deck, spilling jujubes and skinning her knee on the wet sandpapery texture of the deck flooring. She didn't cry, but sat stunned. The little boy stopped too and crouched to study her bloody, abraded skin. Alan offered his clean handkerchief. The girl accepted it with a shy, 'Thanks, mister.' Together Alan and the boy kicked the spilled candy off the side of the boat. Leaning on her little brother, the child limped away; Alan's handkerchief tied sloppily around her knee.

She'd reminded Alan of Delilah with her messy black hair and her suffering in silence. Delilah's silence was one of Alan's favorite things. She didn't even hum when she thought herself alone. When he'd first met her—she was working in the botanical garden where he walked at lunch—he'd thought she might be mute. But no, she was silent by nature. She was one of those who preferred action to words, quick decision to rumination. Alan wondered what action she'd take when he told her his news. He threw his empty cup in the trash and sat down again. The bench was damp from the spray, but he'd given his handkerchief away so he'd just have to deal with a wet ass. Teresa would say he was risking piles.

Teresa was a talker. Teresa believed every possible outcome should be discussed, no, analyzed before decisions were made and outcomes revealed. Last night, Teresa told Alan he could lose Delilah or he could lose his family. Teresa made it very clear and then she stopped talking. That's when Alan knew she was serious. A quiet Teresa was a scary Teresa.

Now, Alan needed to make a decision and he had until he reached Delilah to do it. Did he want to give up Delilah? Did he want to give up his marriage? His children were grown and he thought Teresa had raised them to be reasonable people— surely he wouldn't lose them? If he gave up Delilah to keep Teresa would Teresa forgive him? And forget his trespass against her? She'd forgiven him in the past, but he'd never bought anyone a beach cottage before. He wasn't sure Teresa could ever forgive him a trespass on the scale of real estate. Some things just couldn't be forgotten.

'Alan Trier?' the sheriff had asked.

'Yes, good to meet you.' Alan extended his hand. The sheriff didn't take it. The ferry was emptying around them. Alan was waiting his turn to drive forward.

'I'm the sheriff here,' the sheriff said. 'We need to talk.'

'Is everything all right?'

'We need to talk.' The sheriff looked off toward the end of the line of vehicles waiting to disembark. The wind was lifting his hair from his scalp.

'May I ask what this is about?' Alan inched the car forward. The other man took two steps to stay abreast of the Porsche's window.

'There are some official questions that need answering.' The sheriff bit off his words. He looked inexplicably angry. Alan worried that Teresa was behind this somehow, but then dismissed that as paranoia.

'What questions?' Alan asked. 'About what? Is Delilah okay?'

As his representative on the island, maybe that

should have been his first question. Or maybe, his paranoia reasserted itself, he shouldn't have mentioned her at all. But what else could this be about? It wasn't even Friday, he'd never been here mid-week. Most of the vehicles surrounding him seemed to be service trucks. Except there was the little girl and boy he'd met earlier in the station wagon ahead of him. The little boy was asleep, his head slumped corpse-like on his mother's shoulder, his opened mouth stained red with jujubes. The little girl waved Alan's bloody borrowed handkerchief goodbye as the line finally moved off the ferry at a brisk pace.

Alan waved back and the sheriff whirled to see at whom. The man's body wilted in disappointment. Alan started to worry.

'What is this about?' Alan asked, his foot on the brake. 'Where is Delilah?'

The sheriff's arms dropped to his sides and he slapped his left hand against his thigh. 'Meet me at the cottage,' was all he said before he walked off the ferry's deck.

At the cottage, Alan didn't let him in. He wanted answers, not an interrogation. When Sheriff Ted told him Delilah was gone, the man next door was gone, and a federal marshal was asking after them both—Alan's paranoia said to him, *See? I told you.*

'What is Delilah's real name?' Ted asked.

'Delilah Artemisia Ortiz,' Alan said. They were standing on the porch. Alan hadn't tried the door yet, and overgrown rosemary branches were beating both of them about the knees from the force of the wind.

'No,' Sheriff Ted said. 'Her real name. What's her real name?'

'What?' Alan asked while his paranoia said *Whoa, didn't see that one coming.*

'The marshal looked her up. Or tried to.' Ted looked desperate now, no longer angry. 'There is no Delilah Ortiz. We need to know her real name.'

'Delilah,' Alan repeated. 'Her name is Delilah.'

Ted was disgusted. 'You don't know anything either. That's it. They're just gone.'

'Who's "they"?' Alan, feeling stupid and stymied and agitated, kicked the rosemary bush. Bees shot out of it in alarm. Both men skidded off the porch to end by the gate, outside on the graveled driveway. For the first time Alan noticed that in the garden things were dusty, wilted, thirsty looking. How long had she been gone?

'Delilah and the man next door. The marshal won't tell me his name.' Again, the sheriff wasn't angry. He was desperate, worried. Alan's paranoia didn't like this. 'Mrs. Oakapple next door and Mrs. Bradshaw down the street saw Delilah get into the car of the man next door, and Jack Silva, the dockmaster, loaded them on. After that, who knows?'

The sheriff wasn't reading this information from a notebook, he recited it from memory and then ran one hand violently through his gray hair.

'What's this to you?' Alan asked. His inner voice yelled, *Are you crazy? The sheriff has a gun!*

But the sheriff didn't get angry. He calmed down and gave Alan a look. The look reminded Alan of the way his accountant looked at him after discussing the housekeeping receipts of two households, two women. The look said, *You think you're getting away with something, but God you're a dumb schmuck.* Alan didn't want either man's pity or approbation, but this man *was* wearing a gun.

'I'm the sheriff on this island,' Ted said wearily. 'When a federal marshal comes looking for someone, it's only polite to involve me.'

'Why would a marshal look for Delilah?' Alan asked. 'And her name *is* Delilah.'

'Not Delilah,' the sheriff was impatient at this point. He wanted away. 'The neighbor. The man in the car.' Ted thumbed over his shoulder at the yellow house looming above them. Alan looked up at it, and Ted sighed before handing Alan a card.

'You don't know any more than the rest of us,' Ted said. 'If she contacts you, call that number on the card. I'll get the message.'

Without another word, the sheriff walked away to his car. Alan went inside the unlocked house, checked every room and closet, and then found the note on the mantel. The sight of it caused him to slump upon the nearest piece of furniture and slip into an impromptu slumber.

There was a flutter, a bird's unfamiliar cry, and Alan awoke from a sleep he didn't know he'd slipped into. It was full daylight and the windows were open, the white curtains moving in the breeze that smelled like saltwater and something herby. Rosemary? There was a bird, a small tawny thing, clinging to the screen with its claws. Her wings were beating against the net to maintain balance and it was this noise that Alan heard like a foreign heartbeat.

He was not in the bedroom. He'd fallen asleep on the uncomfortable, minimally padded wooden divan in the living room of the cottage he'd bought for Delilah. The walls, floors, and ceiling were all painted a pearly white. The curtains now whipping through the room as the wind picked up were white, and what little furniture the room contained was either plain sanded wood or painted in pastel colors. In consequence, the room reflected so much light Alan couldn't believe he'd fallen asleep—let alone deep enough to dream.

He couldn't remember the dream, only the feeling of it. Some kind of loss, or he was alone and in danger. He'd misplaced something or he'd been misplaced. He wasn't even looking for it, whatever it was, in the dream. He was mourning what was lost. This dream possessed the subtlety of a hammer.

The rosemary scent intensified with the wind. The sun must be shining on the bush outside the window covered with purple blossoms; it grew all along the porch steps. Alan had brushed up against it when he'd entered the house that morning. The door was unlocked, waiting for him. Maybe the smell was on him, not coming through the window? Maybe both. Concentrating on the scent meant Alan didn't have to think about the folded white paper behind the green-glass oil lantern on the stone fireplace mantel.

When Alan stopped thinking about the rosemary lingering on his jeans he'd have to get up, read the note and think about what it said. He'd have to read what Delilah wanted to tell him.

He'd have to know what she'd done, where she'd gone, and with whom. Quite frankly, Alan didn't want to know. Not any of it.

But that sheriff wanted to know. If he'd followed Alan into the house, the way he'd obviously wanted to, the note would have been opened and read by now. Alan wouldn't allow that. Alan couldn't read what was undoubtedly a 'Dear John' letter with another man watching. Especially not this man. Sheriff Ted. Alan knew he wasn't the most perceptive man—Teresa told him this at least once a week—but Sheriff Ted wasn't hiding his personal interest in Delilah's whereabouts and well-being.

Alan thought back over the times this summer when Delilah didn't answer the telephone or seemed reticent about her habits, actions, or plans. Alan, appreciating her silence, her discretion, hadn't pried. He'd just gone on living his unperceptive life, thinking of himself, his happiness; living every man's dream. Two women, two households; any half-assed fool would have known that couldn't last. The sheriff seemed to know. When Alan hadn't taken him seriously at first, he'd looked ready to arrest him. Or shoot him. Alan, after his mind-clearing nap, didn't blame him.

Delilah was gone. Her closet was empty, her suitcase and overnight bag were not there, and the refrigerator was clean. All the garbage had been carried out to the curb. Sheriff Ted pointed out that the cottage and the yellow house were sharing a garbage can. This seemed to really upset the sheriff. With that realization, Alan got off the uncomfortable divan and went to read the note left behind the green-glass lantern. The scent of rosemary followed him.

When Alan read the letter, he understood why the sheriff hadn't insisted on searching Delilah's cottage. He'd already done so. He'd read the note, he'd seen the initial D signed at the bottom. He'd no doubt discovered that the journal and Farmer's Almanac normally kept in her bedside table drawer were missing. For all Alan knew, Sheriff Ted was intimately acquainted with every nook and cranny of Delilah's (or whatever her name was) cottage. She hadn't bothered to write them separate goodbye notes.

Thanks for everything! I'll miss you. Water the garden until the house sells, please, Ted. The keys and legal papers are in the desk drawer, Alan. So are the gardening books I've borrowed. Don't worry about me, we'll be fine. All the best, Love! D.

Alan read the note again. He then went outside to the detached garage, where he hadn't bothered to park his car, and looked for the fireproof lockbox Delilah kept on the lowest, darkest shelf of her cobwebbed potting table. He'd given her the box their first Christmas together (well, day after Christmas) to replace the shabby cardboard box in which she'd kept her family photographs, birth certificate, and the newspaper clippings from the scandal of Delilah's father, a Texas police officer, killing her mother before vanishing South. Alan remembered Delilah expressing a strange pleasure in the fact that the garage was so far from the cottage. Alan hadn't paid much attention to her pleasure.

Alan had never seen the photographs or read the clippings Delilah kept in the box. Nor had he seen the birth certificate. Delilah told him her family story once, accepted the lockbox with gracious thanks, and stored it as far as possible from where she slept. The box was gone from the garage.

Only displaced sandy dust smeared across the shelf gave evidence that it had ever been there. No doubt this detail would help the sheriff and the marshal. No doubt this was the kind of information the sheriff was asking for, figurative hat in hand. He wanted Delilah's origin story. But Alan was damned if he would be the one to give it to them. She would always be Delilah to him.

Alan collected the keys, legal documents and the books, and then he left to catch the last ferry off the island. He took the books to the sheriff's station—Ted's name was written on the flyleaf—with the note tucked inside one of them. The deputy at the counter flipped open the cover of the top book.

'Sheriff left a message for you,' the deputy called out, and Alan turned away from the door.

Aside from the woman sitting huddled next to the pot-bellied stove in the corner—the stove wasn't lit because it was the middle of summer, but she was the oldest lady Alan had ever seen upright and was wearing so many layers of clothing that she'd probably reached that age where she was cold all the time—Alan and the deputy were alone. Sitting next to the stove was probably more habit than sense, Alan supposed. He dragged his gaze away from the old lady, whose scarf was printed with red apples, to the deputy who waited for Alan's attention with bovine patience.

'Sheriff said if you stopped in I should tell you—' The deputy paused as the old lady creaked to her feet. Both men watched until she was standing.

'What's the message?' Alan prodded. He didn't

care if the lady heard. She was approaching the counter where they stood.

'That marshal called and said she couldn't give us any information,' the deputy said.

Both men were still watching the old lady walk; this let them avoid each other's eyes while awaiting her eventual arrival. The sheriff's station lobby was not large, but she was incredibly slow.

'That's the message?' Alan asked. '*He* called to say "I can't say anything"?'

'Hmpt,' the old lady agreed with Alan. She finally reached the counter and clung to it for support.

'*She* isn't allowed to share any information,' the deputy went on somewhat desperately. 'But out of professional courtesy, she wanted us to know that we could call off the BOLO.'

'What does that mean?' Alan felt something floating to the surface and he dreaded it.

'Be on the lookout,' the deputy said.

'No,' Alan said. 'I know that. What did that message mean? She can't share any news, but don't be on the lookout?'

The deputy finally met Alan's gaze and then froze in place behind the counter. Something in Alan's demeanor rendered poor Deputy Bob mute. The two men stared at each other in frustrated mutual horror. Alan's vision was blurry. A small gnarled hand, dry and light as an autumn leaf, rested on top of Alan's clenched fist on the counter. He had forgotten about the old lady.

'You stop looking for something, dear,' Mrs. Oakapple said, 'when you've found it.'

Her sympathy undid Alan completely. He turned and left the sheriff's station. The bell hanging from the doorknob rang out once in farewell.

Perhaps one day, Delilah thought as she rode the ferry with Anton, standing in the spray and the sunlight, her back warmed by his front, perhaps she would send postcards back to the island; back to the home she'd created with Anton. Perhaps the postcards would be photographs she would take, photographs of their life. She had packed the Leica Alan gave her for her birthday. Perhaps she'd send him a postcard, too.

For Ted she imagined a garden scene of their home in Prescott, Arizona. No, too arid there and what kind of restaurant would they have for Anton? Not the desert Southwest. A garden needed rain. Delilah would send Ted a postcard of her garden in the Pacific Northwest. Redwoods and ferns and mosses would be the underpinnings, the bones she would grow her masterpiece upon.

She had read that hydrangeas grew to epic proportions in Washington State. Ted would be proud of her and her giant blue hydrangeas.

To Maisie Thompson, her friend and sparring partner, Delilah would send a postcard of all the pretty appliances in her kitchen. A kitchen decorated and maintained by Delilah. She imagined mopping a black-and-white checkered floor before Anton turned her in his arms to slip his hands on either side of her jaw and kiss her lightly again and again. Anton would use the clean kitchen to cook the meals eaten by their children. Then Delilah sent a mental photograph of her children to Maisie as well. They looked like her but with Anton's sweet disposition.

Perhaps Delilah would send her baby announcements to Alan and Teresa, too. *See what I made!* Maybe that would be cruel, but more likely they wouldn't care. Delilah wondered if she would spend the rest of her life questioning—when she wasn't raising her family, gardening, or helping Anton run his restaurant—whether or not Alan had ever really cared. Maybe she was just another pretty, high-status plaything like his Porsche or that stallion he didn't know how to ride.

Then Anton tilted her face to kiss her below her ear, down her jawbone to the corner of her mouth, and all thoughts of anyone other than

Anton stopped. When their lips separated, swollen and tender, Delilah looked him in the eye and would have asked 'Alan who?' if asked about her former lover. When Anton looked back she saw in his expression everything she had ever looked for, but not found, in anyone else's. She saw homes, not houses; station wagons, not sports cars; partnership not mentorship. She found Anton looking at her bare, open face with something like awe in his eyes. He tucked the wind-blown hair behind her ears, kissed her gently once more and then asked, 'Should we have a snack before we disembark?' And Delilah melted.

She sent a postcard to her *abuela* in heaven, right then. She sent a photograph of Anton looking at her so lovingly, wanting to feed her before taking her away from here. Anton, dirty kitchen and all, was the *novio* Abuela had always dreamed of for her granddaughter. This postcard was signed 'Dolores'.

The Village

The summer ended and a short intense autumn saw the village residents through what they came to realize was collective shock. Immediately after the disappearance and a round of fact-sharing (it wasn't gossip—they were genuinely concerned for the girl's well-being and the sheriff's sanity—and conjecture wasn't helpful to either) the islanders stopped discussing what happened in those houses, that driveway. What good would discussion do?

Gone was gone and their sturdy fortitude didn't believe in wishful thinking. Those so inclined spared a few moments to pray for the girl, whatever her name might be. She'd need their prayers running off with that Mafia-type. Alan, they didn't give much thought to, a married man making a fool of himself and in that silly car, too. Anton's ancient Renault was more the island men's speed, but they never did learn his name. No one thought of Alan after sharing the story of his departure from the sheriff's station. But a few of the women, led by Mrs. Oakapple, did throw out a wish or two for his wife. They wished her well, but they also wished for her to give Alan hell.

By fall's end the villagers, starting with the older women, forgave the sheriff what they saw as his temporary lapse of judgment. He was lonely, the women said. Who could resist her? The men of Ted's generation shrugged. The men of Delilah's age didn't say anything; they were still pretty resentful.

'If I had known she was looking for someone to run off with, I'd have tried to talk to her,' said Ray Ramirez, but then looked over his shoulder in case his wife or mother or teenaged son or the sheriff was near. His friends checked too, but no one laughed. No one wanted to laugh at Ted. And they didn't want him to see their pity. But he wasn't there behind them. Ted was keeping to himself.

Ted was keeping busy preparing his garden for the winter. The dead annuals were cut back, pulled out, or mulched over. Any late seeds were saved. The buddleia bushes were cut almost to the ground. They only bloom on new growth and Ted intended to have a bumper crop of sweet-smelling purple blossoms when the time came. He needed something to look forward to. The deep-blue hydrangeas he gave a wide berth. Those were on their own.

The rose bushes, trees, and ramblers were trimmed to the point on each branch where leaves of five appeared, but not yet swathed in burlap, and loosely tied to prevent the strong Atlantic winds from ripping them away. It was too soon to cover them. Ted was starting his clean-up early because, once he finished his own garden, he fully intended to go put Delilah's garden to bed. He didn't care what the marshal said; she'd always be Delilah to Ted.

Heaping a pine-scented mulch over his raised beds, Ted planned his approach at Delilah's. He'd start out back, covering the baby apple trees and mulching the new herb areas. The wrought-iron patio furniture should be dragged into the detached garage or risk rusting completely in the sea spray gales. By starting in the back, Ted knew, he lessened his chances of exposure.

The houses on either side of the driveway being empty, Mrs. Oakapple was the only neighbor able to overlook Delilah's back garden, and Ted knew she was sympathetic to his cause. She'd had Ray Ramirez deliver a spice cake to Ted's house—not the station. One or two anonymous casseroles had appeared as well, but everyone knew Mrs. Oakapple's nutmeg pound cake. It was as good as a signed confession.

Ted recognized, as he placed newspaper in the path between rows of what had been eggplants, that the cake was the only confession of sympathy he'd ever receive. Delilah's note on the mantel, addressed to no one, meant for everyone, would never be enough for Ted. But he knew Delilah, or he had, maybe. She thought thanks sufficient. She thought the pleasure of her company enough, never realizing that to Ted and possibly Alan—

'That bastard,' Ted said as he stomped the damp paper into place. To Ted the pleasure of her company felt like the promise of a future, not a payment for the past.

Delilah wrote that she would miss him. Ted would like to believe that, but he thought most likely he'd never be able to, not really. Delilah finished her garden and moved on, Ted's theory went. He'd have to take comfort of a sort, a bitter sort, in the thought that he'd helped her. In the future, every time she thought of her island garden she'd also have to think of Ted. Would that be missing him? Ted supposed it depended on how much help Anton gave in her new garden. The marshal, in some strange burst of un-law-enforcement-officer-like pity, similar to the phone call telling Ted to call off the BOLO, had called back again. She had finally given up a name: Anton. Ted didn't know why she'd told him. Maybe the marshal would call again and Ted could ask her. Ted stomped the final piece of damp newspaper into the soil.

He was almost done in his own garden and half the day was left to live through. He was going to go across the island and put Delilah's garden to rest. He'd do what he could for her, still. Maybe the 'miss you' was a sop to his ego on her part, but missing her was quite real for him. Ted would start in the front kitchen garden, he decided. Giving the villagers something to talk about over the icy winter would be just another service their sheriff could provide for them.

Ted wound up the garden hose and placed his shovel carefully on its hook in the shed. He didn't bother to go back inside his quiet house. There was nothing in there that he needed. He hopped into his official cruiser, not his truck, and started across the island to the empty cottage. He would park in the driveway for everyone to see.

The chain and the PRIVATE PROPERTY sign had disappeared with Delilah.

Acknowledgments

Thank you to my mother for giving me life, and buying me books and letting me skip so much school in order to stay home and read them. I write because of you.

Thank you to my husband who makes it possible that I have the luxury of writing time. Thanks for cooking your own meals, explaining power tool functions, and how a carburetor works. (I'll try to forgive you for saying the power tool conversation was the best conversation of our marriage.)

Thank you to Louise Boland and Urska Vidoni, editorial angels. Delilah is better because of you both.

Thank you to Charles Thompson, best friend forever, for reading a short story and saying, 'Oh no, this isn't done.' As always, you were correct.

Thanks for reading the next five drafts as well. Sorry, not sorry.

Thank you to Kit-Bacon Gressitt for reading drafts of this story, and keeping me sane as our country falls apart. The personal is political and vice versa.

Thank you to the University of California, Riverside/Palm Desert Master of Fine Arts Program. Tod Goldberg and Agam Patel created a world where craft, hard work, and equally hard fun made a writing life seem entirely possible. Mary Yukari Waters and Mary Otis not only made me a better writer, but a better woman. Emily Rapp Black taught me to kick ass.

FAIRLIGHT MODERNS

Bookclub and writers' circle notes for all the
Fairlight Moderns can be found at
www.fairlightmoderns.com

SOPHIE VAN LLEWYN

Bottled Goods

When Alina's brother-in-law defects to the West, she and her husband become persons of interest to the secret services, causing both of their careers to come grinding to a halt. As the strain takes its toll on their marriage, Alina turns to her aunt for help – the wife of a communist leader, and a secret practitioner of the old folk ways.

Set in 1970s communist Romania, this novella-in-flash draws upon magic realism to weave a tale of everyday troubles that can't be put down.

'It is a story to savour, to smile at, to rage against and to weep over.'
- Zoe Gilbert, author of *FOLK*

'Sophie van Llewyn has brought light into an era which cast a long shadow.'
- Joanna Campbell, author of *Tying Down the Lion*

KAREN B. GOLIGHTLY

There Are Things I Know

Eight-year-old Pepper sees the world a little differently from most people. One day, during a school field trip, he is kidnapped by a stranger and driven to rural Arkansas. The man who calls himself 'Uncle Dan' claims that Pepper's mother has died and they are to live together from now on – but Pepper isn't convinced.

He's always found it hard to figure out when people are lying, but he's absolutely certain his mother is alive, and he's going to find her...

'Pepper proves a tenacious, resourceful hero.
Immensely readable and sweetly told.'
- Marti Leimbach, bestselling author of *Daniel Isn't Talking*

EMMA TIMPANY

Travelling in the Dark

Sarah is travelling with her young son back to her home town in the South of New Zealand. When debris from an earthquake closes the road before her, she is forced to extend her journey, and divert through the places from her youth that she had hoped never to return to. As the memories of her childhood resurface, she knows that for the sake of her son, she must face up to them now or be lost forever.

'*A tour de force of imagery and emotion.*'
- Clio Gray, author of *The Anatomist's Dream*

ANTHONY FERNER

Inside the Bone Box

*"As he tiptoed his way through the twisting paths
of sulci and fissures and ventricles, he'd play
Bach, something austere yet dynamic."*

Nicholas Anderton is a highly respected neurosurgeon at the top of his field. But behind the successful façade all is not well. Tormented by a toxic marriage, and haunted by past mistakes, Anderton has been eating to forget. His wife, meanwhile, has turned to drink.

There are sniggers behind closed doors – how can a surgeon be fat, they whisper; when mistakes are made and his old adversary Nash steps in to take advantage Anderton knows things are coming to a head...

Anthony Ferner is a former professor of international business and is published widely in non-fiction in his field. He has one other published novella, *Winegarden*.